Schooling

MASCOT MADNESS!

ALSO BY ANDY GRIFFITHS

Around

MASCOT MADNESS!

ANDY GRIFFITHS

SCHOLASTIC INC.
New York   Toronto   London   Auckland   Sydney
Mexico City   New Delhi   Hong Kong   Buenos Aires

ISBN-13: 978-0-439-92619-5
ISBN-10: 0-439-92619-X

12 11 10 9 8 7 6 5 4 3 2 1   9 10 11 12 13 14/0

Printed in the U.S.A.   40

First printing, February 2009

For Sooty

Chapter 1

Once upon a time

Once upon a time there was — and still is — a school called Northwest Southeast Central School.

Northwest Southeast Central School is located to the southeast of a town called Northwest, which is located to the northwest of Central City.

You don't need to know where Central City is, because it's not important. What *is* important is the school. In this school there is a classroom. And in that classroom there is a fifth grade class. Most important of all, in that class of fifth grade students, there is a student named Henry McThrottle who likes to tell stories.

That's where I come in.

I'm Henry McThrottle ... and this is my latest story.

Chapter 2

Milk attack!

It all started one morning before school a few weeks ago.

I was standing in the school yard with my friends Jack Japes, Jenny Friendly, Gretel Armstrong, and Newton Hooton.

Jack was telling us about a fish he'd caught over the weekend. Like most of Jack's fishing stories, it was entertaining, but mostly untrue.

"You should have seen it!" said Jack, spreading his arms as wide apart as he could. "It was *this* big!"

"In your dreams, Jack," said Gretel, rolling her eyes.

"It was no dream!" said Jack. "You should have seen the way it fought! It practically pulled me off the boat and down into the water!"

Newton gasped with fright.

Newton was always gasping with fright.

Newton was scared of . . . well, pretty much everything, I guess.

You name it, he was scared of it. He was even

scared of the word *it* on the grounds that you could never be quite sure what *it* referred to.

"Don't worry, Newton," I said, patting him on the shoulder. "Jack's just exaggerating."

"No," said Newton, shaking his head. "I'm not scared of that."

"Then what are you scared of?" I said.

"THAT!" said Newton, pointing behind me.

"Uh-oh," said Gretel.

"Uh-oh," said Jack.

"Watch out, Henry!" said Jenny.

I turned around to see the Northwest West Academy bus roaring past the school. I also saw an object being thrown from one of the windows of the bus, and the next thing I knew I was covered in milk.

Sweet, sticky, banana-flavored milk.

"See you at the games, Northwest Southeast Central losers!" yelled the familiar voice of Northwest West Academy school president, Troy Gurgling. Then the bus disappeared in gales of laughter and a cloud of black, foul-smelling smoke.

I stood there, dripping with milk.

"Are you all right, Henry?" said Jenny with a worried look on her face.

"Yeah, I'm fine, thanks," I said. "Just a bit more banana-milky than usual, I guess."

"Do you want me to take you to Mrs. Bandaid?"

Mrs. Bandaid was the school nurse. Her solution to every injury or illness was to apply Band-Aids. Lots of Band-Aids.

"No," I said. "I'm not hurt . . . just a bit sticky."

"A bit *stinky*, you mean," said Fred Durkin, arriving with his brother, Clive.

"Yeah," echoed Clive, "*really* stinky. Good one, Fred!"

"Thanks for your help," said Gretel, stepping in front of them and flexing her muscles. "Now run away and play like good little boys."

"I was just leaving, anyway," said Fred, eyeing Gretel warily. "Something around here stinks like rotten bananas."

"It didn't before you came," said Jack.

Fred glared at Jack. "Why, you little pip-squeak squirt, I'm going to squeeze your head so hard that it pops!"

Gretel stepped in between them, her arms folded across her chest.

Fred stared at Gretel, his eyes narrowed to two black slits. "One of these days, Armstrong," he said quietly, "one of these days . . ."

"You're going to learn some manners?" suggested Gretel.

"No," said Jack, peering out from behind Gretel. "He's going to take a bath!"

Fred stared at Jack.

Jack stared at Fred.

Fred glanced at Gretel.

Gretel jerked her head. "Move it," she said to Fred.

Fred shrugged. "Come on, Clive," he said. "Let's go somewhere where it doesn't stink so much."

Fred turned and walked away.

"Good one, Fred!" said Clive, running after him. "Good one!"

Chapter 3

The Super Dryer 3000

As I walked into the 5B classroom, I wondered how so much milk could have come out of such a small container.

I was soaked. My clothes stuck to me and, as much as I hated to admit it, Fred was right — I stank. Like bananas.

"What happened, Henry?" said Fiona McBrain, looking up from her calculator.

"Northwest West Academy happened," I said, "that's what. They threw a container of milk out of their bus."

"Oh, my goodness," said Fiona. "A missile projected at that velocity could have caused a serious injury! Let me see . . ." She began punching numbers into her calculator, muttering all the while about missiles, trajectories, and projected impacts.

"That's completely out of line!" said David Worthy, who was class president. He was holding the school handbook. "It says here that it's completely against school rules to project missiles from moving vehicles!"

"David," said Gretel, "that's *our* school handbook. The missile was projected by Northwest West Academy. They play by their own rules, remember?"

"Oh, yeah," said David glumly. "I hate it when people play by their own rules."

"Oh, no!" said Penny and Gina. "The horses! We tied them up in the yard. Are they all right?"

Penny and Gina were referring to their imaginary horses. Our teacher, Mr. Brainfright, had insisted they be tethered outside so Penny and Gina could concentrate on their class work.

"They're fine," said Jenny. "They didn't get a drop on them!"

Meanwhile, Grant Gadget said, "Don't worry, Henry — I've got just the thing to dry you off in no time. Stay there!"

Grant dashed out into the corridor to his locker. Grant's dad was an inventor, and Grant was always coming to school with some interesting new invention borrowed from his dad's laboratory. Unfortunately, the inventions didn't always work quite the way they were supposed to. But they were always interesting.

"This ought to be good," said Jack, folding his arms and sucking in his breath. "Glad it's you and not me."

"Well, I've got to do something!" I said. "My clothes feel awful!"

7

"Never fear," said Grant, returning with what looked like an oversize hair dryer, "Grant Gadget is here!"

"That's *exactly* what we fear!" said Jack.

"What I have here," said Grant, ignoring Jack, "is a prototype of the Super Dryer 3000. It's not much bigger than a regular hair dryer, but it has the force — and drying power — of three thousand hair dryers. Are you ready?"

Grant was pointing the Super Dryer 3000 at me, his finger poised on the trigger.

"Don't let him do it, Henry!" warned Jack. "You'll be sorry."

I understood Jack's concern. But I was standing there cold, wet, and smelling of bananas. I figured things couldn't get any worse.

"I'll take my chances, Jack," I said. "Okay, Grant. Let me have it!"

Grant nodded . . . and let me have it.

The Super Dryer 3000 roared to life.

At first it felt like getting blasted by a hair dryer.

Then it felt like getting blasted by three thousand hair dryers.

And then it felt like . . . well, I don't know, because the next thing I knew the sheer force of the Super Dryer 3000 sent me flying backward through the air and out the classroom window!

Chapter 4

Is that delicious smell coming from me?

I ended up lying flat on my back in Mr. Spade's freshly dug flower bed.

Mr. Spade didn't like people falling in his freshly dug flower bed.

I knew this because I could hear him yelling.

I lifted my head out of the soft dirt. Mr. Spade was running toward me, waving his pitchfork.

"Henry?" called Jenny from the window above. "Are you all right?"

"Yes," I called back. "I think so."

"You'd better get out of there," said Gretel. "Mr. Spade's coming."

"And he's got a pitchfork!" said Newton.

"I'm on it," I said, dragging myself out of the dirt with great difficulty. My clothes were dry but now they were all stiff from the dried milk. The sight of the sharp tips of Mr. Spade's pitchfork acted as quite an incentive, though, so I got up and ran.

Luckily, Mr. Spade was still a long way off and I was able to get back to the classroom before he could introduce the tips of his pitchfork to the milk-stiffened seat of my pants.

I had only been back in the classroom long enough for Grant to apologize and explain that the Super Dryer 3000 needed a little work, when Mr. Brainfright entered.

He stopped.

And sniffed.

"Well, I'll be darned," he said, breaking into a huge grin. "Banana! I can smell banana! And it smells as if it's been warmed up or toasted. Lovely!"

Mr. Brainfright liked bananas.

And I don't just mean he liked bananas.

I mean he *really* liked bananas.

He took a few steps toward me, sniffing as he walked. "Henry?" he said. "Is that delicious smell coming from you?"

"Yes, sir!" I said. "But I can explain . . ."

"No need to explain," he said. "Let's just enjoy it! There's nothing quite like the smell of fresh banana in the morning! What a wonderful, wonderful morning!"

"No, it's not," I said, standing there in my stiff, uncomfortable, smelly clothes. "It's a terrible, terrible morning!"

The rest of the class nodded and murmured their agreement.

Mr. Brainfright frowned. "Whatever do you all mean?" he said. "The sun is shining. The birds are singing. The flowers are blooming. And the room smells like warm bananas. Why the long faces?"

"Because it's track-and-field season," said Jack gloomily.

"Track-and-field season!" exclaimed Mr. Brainfright, his eyes shining. "How wonderful! Out there in the fresh air, warm sun, soft grass . . . pushing yourselves to the limit and beyond! Muscles working, sweat on the brow, lungs bursting, the pure primal thrill of the race . . . running, jumping, throwing . . . Ahh! Some of the best days of my life were spent on the track and in the field."

"Maybe that's how it was for you," said Gretel, "but it's not how it is for us. Track and field for us means getting thrashed by Northwest West Academy at the annual interschool competition."

"Oh, come now," said Mr. Brainfright. "Surely it's not that bad!"

"It *is* that bad," I said. "We're hopeless. We lose every year."

"Northwest West Academy is unbeatable," said Jenny.

"Well, you certainly won't beat them with that attitude," said Mr. Brainfright.

"But they've *never* been defeated," said Gretel. "*Ever*! And their principal, Mr. Constrictor, is an *ex-pro wrestler*."

"Good for him," said Mr. Brainfright.

11

"Yeah," said Jack. "Good for him and *bad* for us. He got thrown out of the World Wrestling Federation . . . for attacking a referee."

"That's not very nice," said Jenny, shocked at the thought of anyone attacking anyone, let alone a referee.

Clive jumped to his feet. "It's not true! It was a setup! The referee was attacking *him!*"

"Whatever," said Jack. "The point is, he doesn't play by the rules."

"I'm going to tell my brother you said that," said Clive, "and I can tell you now, he's not going to like it. He's a big wrestling fan. Mr. Constrictor is his hero. Mine, too. They called him The Boa because he could squeeze his opponents so hard they couldn't breathe."

"That's *definitely* not very nice," said Jenny.

"I'll tell you what else is definitely *not* nice," I said to Mr. Brainfright. "You know how most schools have an anti-bullying program? Well, at Northwest West Academy, Mr. Constrictor has set up a *pro*-bullying program to teach them how to bully more effectively! And their mascot is a pit bull terrier named Chomp!"

"Someone in a pit bull terrier suit, you mean?" said Mr. Brainfright.

"No!" said Jenny. "A *real* pit bull terrier. It belongs to Mr. Constrictor. And it's really mean!" Jenny clapped

12

her hand over her mouth. She hated saying anything bad about anyone, even a dog.

"She's right," said Jack. "It's the biggest, meanest, scariest dog you ever saw. Its teeth are really sharp and it's always growling and barking and — "

"Jack," I said, looking across at Newton, who was staring at Jack with his mouth open, "that's enough. You're upsetting Newton."

"Oh, dear," said Mr. Brainfright. "It sounds like you're really up against it, aren't you? But don't give up hope! Talent and skills will eventually win out over brawn."

"But that's just the thing," said Jenny. "We don't have any talent. Or skills."

"I don't believe that for a moment!" said Mr. Brainfright.

"It's true!" said Jack. "Just ask Mr. Grunt. He'll tell you how bad we are. He says that we're the worst school he's ever coached!"

"Oh, come now," said Mr. Brainfright, chuckling. "I'm sure he doesn't really say that."

"He does!" said Newton. "He says we're hopeless!"

Mr. Brainfright stopped smiling. "Let me get this straight," he said. "Mr. Grunt, your gym teacher, told you that you were 'hopeless'?"

"Yes!" said Newton. "He tells us all the time. And he should know — he was in the Olympics."

Mr. Brainfright stroked his chin. "Is that a fact?"

"Yes," said Gretel. "It's pretty much all he talks about . . . besides telling us how hopeless we are."

"Interesting," said Mr. Brainfright. "Very interesting. When do you next have gym class with Mr. Grunt?"

"After lunch," said David.

"Good," said Mr. Brainfright. "I might come down and watch."

Chapter 5

Mr. Grunt

That afternoon we were sitting on the oval while Mr. Grunt paced up and down in front of us with a clipboard in one hand, a stopwatch in the other, and a whistle around his neck.

Mr. Grunt glared at us, raised the whistle to his lips, and blew it.

Loudly.

"Now listen up, you bunch of no-hopers!" he growled, his eyes bugging out like golf balls. "Today we are going to work on the triple jump. It should be easy enough — even for a bunch of losers like you, 5B. You hop, you step, and you jump. Is that clear?"

We all nodded obediently.

Except for Jack, who looked at me with his eyes all bugged out like Mr. Grunt's.

Even though I was a little scared of Mr. Grunt, I couldn't help laughing. Unfortunately, Mr. Grunt caught me.

"Has something I said amused you, McThrottle?" he said, his eyes bulging out even farther.

"No, sir," I said.

"Then what's so funny?" he demanded.

"Nothing, sir!" I said, desperately trying — but not succeeding — to control myself.

"You're right about that!" said Mr. Grunt. "There's nothing funny about the triple jump! And there's nothing funny about the Northwest track-and-field competition, which, in case you've forgotten, is LESS THAN TWO WEEKS AWAY!"

Mr. Grunt yelled the last five words at the top of his voice, which certainly helped to wipe the smile off my face.

His breath was terrible.

It was so bad, in fact, that I was worried I was going to pass out, and I probably would have if Mr. Brainfright hadn't appeared at that moment, distracting Mr. Grunt from his rant.

"Good afternoon, Mr. Grunt," Mr. Brainfright said cheerfully.

Mr. Grunt eyed Mr. Brainfright suspiciously. "Yes?" he said. "Can I help you?"

"No, no," said Mr. Brainfright. "I just thought I'd come down and see how the class is shaping up for the big competition."

Mr. Grunt's eyes retracted back into his head and narrowed. "You may *watch*, Brainfright, but I'm warning you right now — don't interfere! I'm using cutting-edge training techniques here. I was in the Olympics, you know!"

"Yes, so I've heard," said Mr. Brainfright. "That's exactly why I was hoping you might let me observe — I'm always interested in seeing a master at work in his or her chosen field!"

Mr. Grunt was clearly pleased with Mr. Brainfright's flattery. He puffed out his chest. "I was just teaching them about the triple jump."

"Ah, yes, the triple jump!" said Mr. Brainfright. "It used to be called hop, step, and jump when I was in school."

"Yes, I'm well aware of that," said Mr. Grunt quickly. "It's true that it involves a hop, a step, and a jump — but in order to reduce confusion, they renamed it the triple jump."

Jack put his hand up. "Excuse me, Mr. Grunt," he called out.

"What is it, Japes?" said Mr. Grunt impatiently. He didn't like being interrupted.

"Why is it called the triple jump when there's only *one* actual jump in it?"

Mr. Grunt stared at Jack, his eyes beginning to bug out again. "Japes," he said, "you are a complete idiot!"

I glanced at Mr. Brainfright, who was looking quite shocked. "Mr. Grunt," he said, "I really must protest. I can't see how calling a student a 'complete idiot' is a cutting-edge training technique — "

"It's also against the school rules," said

17

David, holding up the school handbook. "It says here that — "

"Shut it, Worthy," said Mr. Grunt. "I'm not interested in your stupid book. I'm interested in results." Then he turned to Mr. Brainfright. "Who's the expert, here, Brainfright? You or me?"

"You, of course — " said Mr. Brainfright.

"Darn right I am," snapped Mr. Grunt. "And I'll thank you to remember it and keep your own mouth shut, too!"

We had never heard a teacher speak like that to another teacher. And neither, obviously, had Mr. Brainfright, who was so taken aback that he just nodded . . . with his mouth shut.

Mr. Grunt blew his whistle loudly.

"Japes!" he barked. "Since you know so much about the triple jump, you can go first!"

Jack shrugged, got up, and walked to the white line in front of the sandpit. Then he took a deep breath, furrowed his brow, and leaned forward.

"Stop wasting time and do it!" yelled Mr. Grunt.

"Yes, sir!" said Jack.

He ran.

At the white line he stopped running, and with his arms bent and hands floppy in front of him, he did three bouncy jumps. Like a rabbit.

Everybody laughed. Even Mr. Brainfright.

The only person who didn't laugh was Mr. Grunt. "You are a complete waste of space, Japes," he barked. "Fifty laps of the track! Get going!"

"Did I do something wrong?" said Jack.

"No, but I will if you don't get going right now!" said Mr. Grunt, advancing toward him.

Jack ran.

Chapter 6

The handbook toss

"Excuse me, Mr. Grunt," said David, "but was that a threat? Because in the school handbook it says that teachers are not allowed to threaten students."

"Does it really?" said Mr. Grunt, walking across to David.

"It certainly does," said David, pulling his handbook out of his shorts. "It says so right here — section three, subparagraph two!"

"How interesting!" said Mr. Grunt. "May I see that?"

"Yes, sir," said David, handing the book to Mr. Grunt. "Section three, subparagraph two — "

Mr. Grunt took the book and hurled it clear across the field. "No reading in gym class! Do I make myself clear?"

"Yes, sir," said a clearly stunned David.

"Good," said Mr. Grunt. "Then let's get on with it, shall we?"

David nodded.

The only person who looked more stunned than David was Mr. Brainfright. Although no great fan of rule books himself, he always spoke very gently to us. Unless he was shouting, of course, but even then, he managed to shout very gently.

Mr. Grunt looked at us.

We all tried our best to make ourselves invisible, but Newton, who was shaking like a leaf, was the least successful.

"Hooton!" said Mr. Grunt.

"Don't worry, Newton," I whispered. "Just a hop, a step, and a jump, and you'll be fine."

Newton nodded, trying to take in my words. "A jump . . . a hop . . . a step . . . no — hang on — a hop, a jump, and a step? Or was it a hop, a jump, another hop, and a step?"

Mr. Grunt blasted his whistle twice. "Hop to it!" he yelled. "We don't have all day. The competition is in less than two weeks and the clock is ticking!"

Newton ran to the starting line, but he didn't hop.

Or step.

Or jump.

He just kept on running.

And running.

And running.

Clear across the field and back to the locker rooms.

Mr. Grunt watched him and then turned to us. "Well, he's a washout at the triple jump," he said, "but the boy can run, I'll give him that."

"Should I go and see if he's all right?" I said, hoping that it would get me out of having to demonstrate my own complete lack of skill at the triple jump.

But Mr. Grunt had other ideas.

"And miss out on your chance to impress us all with your triple jump, McThrottle?" he said with a mean glint in his bulging eyes. "I don't think so. Up you go."

"But . . ." I protested.

"Do it!" barked Mr. Grunt. "Or do you want to join your friend Jack?"

I looked across at Jack. He was only on his third lap and he was already swaying and stumbling and holding his stomach. He made the triple-jump option look pretty good.

Chapter 7

A stumble, a trip, and a fall

Mr. Grunt blew his whistle. "On your mark, McThrottle!" he said. "Ready, set, go!"

I didn't need any further encouragement; I went.

I ran up and attempted a triple jump.

I was doing okay, too, but somehow, in midair, between the hop and the step, or perhaps the step and the jump — I couldn't be sure — I lost my balance and ended up sprawled face-first in the sand.

"Hopeless!" yelled Mr. Grunt. "Absolutely hopeless! It's called the *triple* jump, remember? There's a *hop*, a *step,* and a *jump*, not a stumble, a trip, and a fall!"

"I'm sorry, Mr. Grunt," I said, "but I — "

But before I could finish, Mr. Grunt blew his whistle.

"Don't give me excuses, McThrottle!" he yelled. "I don't want excuses! I want results! Show me a man who's good at making excuses and I'll show you a LOSER!"

"But Mr. Grunt," I said, "I — "

23

Mr. Grunt blew his whistle again. "What are you, McThrottle?" he said. "A winner or a loser?"

I took a deep breath. "I'm a winner, sir."

"No, you're not," said Mr. Grunt. "Take a look at yourself, McThrottle! You're lying facedown in the sandpit, crying for your mommy —"

"I'm not crying," I said, getting to my knees and blinking as hard as I could. "I've got sand in my eyes and it's making them water!"

"Awwww," said Mr. Grunt. "Poor widdle baby . . . has poor widdle Henry-wenry got sand in his eyes?"

"Now, just a moment!" said Mr. Brainfright, emerging from his shocked silence. "I may not know as much as you but . . ."

"No!" said Mr. Grunt, "You're right. NOBODY knows as much as me!" He pushed past Mr. Brainfright on his way to the starting line. "Get out of my way. I'm going to show you no-hopers how it's done. Look and learn!"

I got up out of the sand as Mr. Grunt crouched down into the starting position. I walked across to where the rest of the class were standing.

"Don't listen to him, Henry," whispered Jenny. "I thought your jump was excellent."

"Thanks," I said.

"No talking!" yelled Mr. Grunt. "I'm trying to concentrate!"

Mr. Grunt blew his whistle twice and then took off.

24

He hopped, stepped, jumped, and, most impressive of all, landed on his feet.

He got up and turned to us with his hands on his hips. "Well?" he said.

We stared back at him.

"Well?" he said again. "I would have thought that at least deserves a round of applause."

We all applauded.

We were too scared not to.

Mr. Grunt did it again.

And again.

And again.

Half an hour later our hands were sore from clapping.

"I think they've got the hang of it now, Mr. Grunt," said Mr. Brainfright.

"I'll tell you when they've got the hang of it!" said Mr. Grunt, walking back to the starting line to do it yet again.

I looked at Jack, who was still doing laps.

He was bent over, panting, and looking like every step was going to be his last.

If only he'd known how lucky he was.

Chapter 8

Debriefing

Back in class, Mr. Brainfright stood at the front of the room, shaking his head. "See what we mean?" said Gretel. "We're useless!"

"And Mr. Grunt is like that all the time?" said Mr. Brainfright.

"It depends how badly we perform," said Gretel. "Today he was in a pretty good mood!"

"That's a good mood?" said Mr. Brainfright. "I can hardly believe it! In all my years of teaching I have never . . . well . . . never mind. We must deal with the problem at hand."

"How to improve our triple jump?" said Jenny.

"No," said Mr. Brainfright.

"Northwest West Academy?" suggested David.

"No," said Mr. Brainfright.

"Mr. C-C-Constrictor?" stammered Newton. He was even scared to say the name.

"Wrong again," said Mr. Brainfright.

Newton shrugged. "It figures. I'm always messing up."

"*That's* the problem!" said Mr. Brainfright.

Newton looked shocked.

"You think *Newton* is the problem?" said Jenny.

"No, no, no," said Mr. Brainfright. "It's what Newton said: 'I'm always messing up.' Mr. Grunt seems to be doing his level best to convince you all that you're losers. I don't think there's anything wrong with you — or the rest of the school, probably — that a good dose of self-esteem and positive thinking wouldn't fix."

"I don't think that's the problem," said Fiona. "Personally, I have very high self-esteem. Northwest West Academy is simply unbeatable — *that's* the problem!"

"No, Fiona," said Mr. Brainfright. "Even you could do with a morale boost! Tell me, what is the Northwest Southeast Central School mascot?"

"We don't have one," I said.

"You don't?" said Mr. Brainfright, brightening. "Well, don't worry! I've got just the thing!"

"What is it?" I asked.

Mr. Brainfright winked. "Top secret," he said, tapping the side of his nose. "I'll bring it in tomorrow."

At that moment Jack staggered into the classroom, looking like death after his fifty laps.

"Did I miss anything?" he said.

"No," said Mr. Brainfright, unable to contain his excitement. "Not yet!"

Chapter 9

Big, yellow, and banana-shaped

The next morning we were sitting in class waiting for Mr. Brainfright to arrive.

Clive Durkin was flicking spitballs.

Jack was drawing a cartoon featuring a giant spitball that looked a lot like Clive.

Newton was looking worried.

Jenny was kneeling beside his desk, comforting him.

Gina and Penny were playing with their toy horses — braiding their colorful manes.

Suddenly, the door of the classroom burst open.

"YIKES!" yelled Newton.

Coming through the doorway was a banana.

A big, yellow, *dancing* banana.

I know that sounds crazy, but I don't know how else to describe it.

It was big.

It was yellow.

It was banana-shaped.

And it was dancing.

It was definitely a big, yellow, dancing banana.

We all sat there and stared. Well, all except for Newton, who dived underneath his desk.

It's not every day that a big, yellow, dancing banana comes into your classroom. But before David could get his handbook out to check whether big, yellow, dancing bananas were permitted in the school, the banana launched into a series of backflips, somersaults, and cartwheels.

It cartwheeled three times across the front of the classroom, along the row of desks beside the windows, across the back of the classroom, up the other side, across the front again, and then went straight out the window!

Everyone sat there staring.

Everyone, that is, except for Jack. "Did a big, yellow, dancing banana just cartwheel around the classroom and fall out the window?" he asked, rubbing his eyes.

"I think so," I said.

"Good," he said. "For a moment there I thought I was seeing things."

"I'm scared," whimpered Newton from underneath his desk.

I knew how he felt. The sight of a giant banana brought back a flood of bad memories . . . memories that I would sooner have forgotten.

"I'm confused," said Fiona, which was unusual because she was so smart that she was rarely confused about anything. "What was a giant banana doing in our classroom? And why was it doing cartwheels?"

"I didn't know bananas could even *do* cartwheels," said Gretel.

"Or somersaults," said Grant.

"We should see if it's all right," said Jenny, getting up and going to the window. She leaned out. "Are you okay?" she called.

"Yes, I'm fine, thank you," called a voice from below.

"That's weird," said Clive. "It sounds just like Mr. Brainfright."

"That's because it *is* Mr. Brainfright!" said Gretel.

"But what's Mr. Brainfright doing in a banana suit?" said Newton.

"Let's ask him and find out," I said.

"Mr. Brainfright, why are you wearing a banana suit?" Jenny called out.

"This isn't just a banana suit," Mr. Brainfright called back. "Meet the new Northwest Southeast Central mascot!"

Chapter 10

An inspiring mascot?

After Mr. Brainfright made his way back into class and took off the suit, he told us all about it.

"I think this is the solution to your athletic problems," he said, holding up the suit. "An inspiring mascot!"

"I can see that a bright, colorful mascot could act as a rallying agent for our school and could encourage and inspire us," said Fiona. "But a banana?"

"Yes, a banana," said Mr. Brainfright. "Believe me, nothing will strike fear into the heart of your opponent more than the sight of a giant banana."

"*Confuse* them, more like," said Jack.

"Even better," said Mr. Brainfright. "A confused opponent is a weakened opponent."

Chapter 11

Mr. Brainfright's important lesson no. 1

Nothing will strike fear into the heart of your opponent more than the sight of a giant banana.

Chapter 12

Mr. Brainfright's important lesson no. 2

A confused opponent is a weakened opponent.

Chapter 13

Who wants to be the banana?

"You really like bananas, don't you, Mr. Brainfright?" said Jenny.

"What's not to like?" said Mr. Brainfright. "They are bright and cheerful in color, easy to peel, and taste great. *Plus* they're good for you."

"But where did you get a *banana* suit?" said Gretel.

"I found it!" said Mr. Brainfright.

"You *found* a banana suit?" said Gretel.

"Yes!" Mr. Brainfright beamed. "It was one of the happiest days of my life! I was taking a shortcut across a vacant lot and I found the suit lying in a puddle. I took it home, cleaned it up, and it was as good as new. Why anybody would want to throw away a perfectly good banana suit is completely beyond me!"

It wasn't beyond me, though.

I knew exactly how it got there.

And to tell you the truth, I would have been happy to never see it again.

Mr. Brainfright held it up. "So," he said, "who

34

wants to be the banana and inspire Northwest Southeast Central School to victory?"

We all looked at each other.

"Hmm," said Mr. Brainfright. "Well, what about you, Gretel?"

"No, we can't spare Gretel," said David. "We need her for the shot put, javelin, and discus."

"Then how about you, David?"

"Oh, no, sir," said David. "I'm a long-distance runner and I also do the long jump. I don't think I could do those in a banana suit."

"Good point," said Mr. Brainfright, looking around the room. "Penny and Gina. Are either of you interested?"

"No, Mr. Brainfright," said Gina. "We do the hurdles."

"Our horses love the hurdles," said Penny.

"Grant?" said Mr. Brainfright.

"Pole vault," said Grant.

"Jenny?"

"Relay, sir."

"Jack?"

"Um, er," said Jack, "I have to focus on my event."

"Which is?" said Mr. Brainfright.

"Triple jump," said Jack with a perfectly straight face.

The class laughed.

Jack grinned. "What about you, Henry?" he said, deflecting attention from himself.

"No," I said. "I can't."

"Do you have a special event?" Mr. Brainfright asked me.

"Yes," I lied. "I have to do a sports report for the school newsletter." Well, it wasn't really a lie — it was the truth, although it wasn't the *whole* truth about why I couldn't possibly be the banana mascot.

"What's the matter, Henry?" said Jenny. "You turned red!"

"Oh," I said, "did I? It's very hot in here. . . ."

"But the windows are wide open!" said Jack.

"I can vouch for that!" said Mr. Brainfright.

Chapter 14

Mr. Brainfright inspires the school

"So," said Mr. Brainfright, "*nobody* wants to be the banana mascot?" He looked around the room.

Nobody volunteered.

Especially not me.

"Well," he said with a big smile, "I guess that leaves me!"

Despite Mr. Brainfright's attempts to find a volunteer, I got the feeling that he wasn't too disappointed to be getting back into the suit.

"Can somebody do the zipper up at the back?" he said.

Jenny jumped up, zipped the suit, and Mr. Brainfright immediately began singing, "If you're a banana and you know it, clap your hands!"

None of us clapped, though.

We just stared.

If you've never seen your teacher in a banana suit singing "If you're a banana and you know it, clap your hands!" — let me tell you that it's a pretty bizarre sight.

But our staring and non-clapping didn't seem to dampen Mr. Brainfright's enthusiasm. "If you're a banana and you know it, clap your hands!" he sang.

He looked so ridiculous that I had to laugh . . . and clap. Jenny joined in. So did Jack.

"If you're a banana and you know it, then you really ought to show it," sang Mr. Brainfright loudly. "If you're a banana and you know it, clap your hands!"

Gretel and Newton joined in, followed by Fiona, David, and Grant. By the time Mr. Brainfright had started the second round, everyone but Clive was clapping.

"You know one of the other things that I love about bananas?" said Mr. Brainfright, after we'd sung the song for a third time.

"What?" said Jack.

"The word is so much fun to spell!"

"I *love* spelling!" said Fiona excitedly.

Mr. Brainfright wrote it up on the board. "Say it with me," he said, pointing to each letter as we chanted it.

"B-a-n-a-n-a-s."

"Good!" boomed Mr. Brainfright. "Again . . . but louder this time!"

"B-A-N-A-N-A-S!" we yelled.

"THAT'S RIGHT!" yelled Mr. Brainfright, jumping and punching his fist into the air. "LET'S GO . . .

BANANAS! Now, get up and say it all together: B-A-N-A-N-A-S . . . LET'S GO . . . BANANAS! B-A-N-A-N-A-S . . . LET'S GO . . . BANANAS! B-A-N-A-N-A-S . . . LET'S GO . . . BANANAS!"

By this time we were all out of our chairs, jumping, punching the air, and yelling "B-A-N-A-N-A-S . . . LET'S GO . . . BANANAS!" as loud as we could. We made a mess of the spelling, but nobody was in doubt about the feeling behind it.

"This is really fun!" said Jenny.

"I feel great!" said Jack.

"Me too!" said Newton, who for once wasn't looking scared at all.

"This is all highly irregular," shouted David above the noise. He had his handbook open in front of him and was pointing at a page. "Section thirty-one, subparagraph three specifically forbids chanting in class."

"It most certainly DOES!" yelled Mrs. Cross, who was standing in the doorway with her hands on her hips, but before she could tell Mr. Brainfright to control his class and stop making so much noise, she stopped and stared at the giant banana that was dancing and singing and pointing at the letters on the blackboard.

"Oh, hello, Mrs. Cross!" said Mr. Brainfright. "Would you be so kind as to point to the letters for me? I'm trying to dance, you see, and the pointing is really cramping my style." And with that, he put the pointer into her hand and guided her to the front of the room.

At first, poor Mrs. Cross was too surprised to do anything but stand there and point, but as the chant continued, an amazing thing began to happen. She softened, relaxed, and the corners of her mouth began to twitch, and spasm, and rise up toward her ears.

"Henry!" cried Newton, alarmed. "Something's wrong with Mrs. Cross!"

I laughed. "There's nothing wrong," I reassured Newton. "She's just smiling."

And soon she was doing a whole lot more than that. She was singing and dancing and chanting along with the rest of us.

If we needed any more proof of the power of Mr. Brainfright's banana suit, the sight of Mrs. Cross kicking her heels up and smiling was it.

But there was more to come.

Plenty more.

Chapter 15

Principal Greenbeard arrives

We had all just formed a conga line behind Mr. Brainfright and were parading and stomping around the room when Principal Greenbeard appeared.

He was all decked out in a brilliant white suit, looking more like the captain of a ship than a school principal.

And there was a good reason for this.

Principal Greenbeard didn't think that he *was* a school principal.

In fact, he didn't even think that the school was a school.

He liked to imagine that the school was a big ship and that he was the captain and the staff and students were all members of the crew.

Principal Greenbeard stood there, trying to make sense of the sight of a giant banana leading a group of students — as well as another teacher — in a crazy, noisy conga-line stomp around the classroom.

"What in the deep blue sea is going on here?" he finally spluttered.

The conga line came to a halt.

41

"Good morning, Principal Greenbeard!" said Mr. Brainfright. "Care to join us in a conga?"

"No, I most certainly do *not*," said Principal Greenbeard. "Who — and what — the devil are you?"

Mr. Brainfright removed the head of his costume. "It's me," he said.

Principal Greenbeard blinked a few times. "Brainfright?" he said.

"Yes! I'm the new Northwest Southeast Central School mascot!"

"I've sailed the seven seas for many years and seen and heard of many strange things," said Principal Greenbeard, "but I've never seen or heard of a banana mascot."

"Of course not," said Mr. Brainfright. "That's why it's going to be so effective! It will confuse Northwest West Academy to no end."

Principal Greenbeard's eyes lit up. "And a confused opponent is a weakened opponent!"

"My thoughts exactly!" said Mr. Brainfright. "Well, what do you think?"

Principal Greenbeard stroked his chin. "Hmmm," he said, "perhaps you're right, Brainfright. There's no denying that Northwest Southeast Central is in the doldrums when it comes to sports. And we've been all at sea for a long time now — maybe a banana mascot is just the thing we need to cure our scurvy!"

42

Chapter 16

Return of Fred and Clive

At lunchtime Gretel, Newton, Jenny, Jack, and I were sitting in our usual spot in the shade beside the basketball court discussing the events of the morning when Fred and Clive appeared.

, "Your teacher's a freak," said Fred.

"No, he's not," said Jack. "He's a banana."

"Sorry," said Fred. "My mistake. He's a banana-shaped freak."

"Good one, Fred," said Clive, slapping his brother on the back.

"If you think your teacher dressing up as a banana is going to help us beat Northwest West Academy, then you're wrong," said Fred. "We haven't got a chance and you know it."

"At least he's trying," said Gretel.

"He can try all he likes," said Fred, "but Northwest Southeast Central School will never beat Northwest West Academy. Not in a million years . . . and not even with a million banana mascots."

"Hey, that's a great idea," said Jack. "A million banana mascots! Imagine that!"

"You can imagine all the banana mascots you like, Japes," said Fred. "Imagine us winning while you're at it. Because that's the only place it's ever going to happen: in your mind!"

"Why are you so negative?" asked Jenny. "Don't you want us to win?"

"Sure I do," said Fred, shrugging. "But we never will. It's not just Northwest West Academy we're up against — it's *The Boa.*"

I rolled my eyes.

"You can't beat The Boa," said Clive. "We've watched all his fights. My dad's got the twenty-DVD set — *The Greatest Wrestlers Ever in the History of the Entire World* — and The Boa takes up nineteen of them. He's a legend."

"Yeah?" said Jack. "Well, if he's such a legend, then how come he was thrown out of the World Wrestling Federation?"

Fred scowled and pointed at Jack angrily. "That was not his fault. It was a frame-up. He was attacked by the referee."

"Oh, really? That's not what I heard," said Jack.

"What did you hear?" said Fred.

"That he started it," said Jack.

"Well, you heard wrong," said Fred. "And if you go around saying that, you'll be sorry."

"Why, what are you going to do?" Gretel challenged. "Tell The Boa?"

We all laughed.

Well, everybody except Fred and Clive.

"I might just do that," said Fred, turning and walking away.

"Yeah," said Clive, trotting after him. "He might just do that."

Chapter 17

The winners' podium

Even if we had a new mascot, we still had to go to the same old gym class. The next morning we were sitting outside on the oval while Mr. Grunt called the roll.

When he finished, he put down his clipboard and gave us a bug-eyed stare. "In case you've forgotten," he said, "the Northwest interschool track-and-field competition is next Friday."

None of us, of course, had forgotten that the Northwest interschool track-and-field competition was next Friday.

"Now," continued Mr. Grunt, "in the unlikely event that any of you losers actually wins an event on the day, you are going to need to know how to stand on a winners' podium without falling off. Do any of you even know what a winners' podium is?"

Fiona put up her hand. "It's a set of three blocks, sir, of varying height. The winner stands on the highest block in the center. The second-place winner stands on a lower block on the winner's right and the third-place winner stands on another lower block on the winner's left. Just like the one behind you, sir."

"Very good, Fiona," said Mr. Grunt. "What a pity your legs don't work as fast as your brain."

Fiona looked outraged. But she didn't dare say anything.

Mr. Grunt went on with his lecture. "Now, you might think that climbing up onto one of these is a simple matter, but it's not as easy as it looks. Even someone as experienced with standing on these as I am can occasionally stumble. I remember when I once won a gold medal for something or other — there've been so many I can barely remember them all . . ."

I rolled my eyes. Mr. Grunt was off on another story about his past sports glories.

". . . as I went to mount the block, the roar of the crowd momentarily disoriented me and I stumbled. Luckily, thanks to my excellent reflexes and finely honed sense of balance, I was able to recover almost instantly, averting what could have turned a sports triumph into nothing more than a highlight on a sports bloopers show."

Clive laughed.

"Something funny, Durkin?" said Mr. Grunt.

"I like bloopers shows," said Clive, still chuckling.

"Well, that doesn't surprise me," said Mr. Grunt. "Bloopers shows are full of losers making mistakes for the amusement of other losers."

Clive stopped laughing. "I'm telling my brother you said that," he muttered.

Mr. Grunt ignored him. "So, since none of you have my great reflexes and finely honed sense of balance, we are going to spend this class practicing how to mount and stand on a winners' podium without falling off." He looked around for a suitable victim. "Hooton, you're first up."

Newton looked worried. "I'd rather not, sir," he said. "I'm scared of heights."

"All the more reason to get up there," said Mr. Grunt. "Fear is your enemy! Obliterate it. Pound it into submission. Show it who's the boss."

"Why are you always picking on Newton?" said Jenny.

"I'm not *picking* on him," said Mr. Grunt. "I'm offering him an opportunity to become a winner."

"Can I just stand on one of the lower blocks, please?" said Newton, pointing to the third-place block.

"Certainly not," said Mr. Grunt. "Third place is no place for winners."

"What about second?" said Newton.

"No! Second place is just another word for first loser," said Grunt. "Get up there, boy. Show me that you're not as pathetic as you look."

Newton rose to his feet unsteadily. Jenny squeezed his hand. "Go on, Newton," she said. "You can do it."

Newton walked tentatively toward the podium and stood in front of it. Then he put his right foot onto the second-place block and climbed up. He stood there, knees shaking. "I think I'm getting a nosebleed. It's the altitude."

"Nonsense, boy — keep climbing," said Mr. Grunt.

Newton put his left foot onto the first-place block.

"I don't want to do this, sir," he whimpered. "I can't . . ."

"You will!" said Mr. Grunt. "Right now!"

Newton did as he was told until he stood shakily on the highest block.

"How do you feel?" asked Mr. Grunt.

"Dizzy," said Newton.

"No wonder," said Mr. Grunt. "Winning is a heady experience, isn't it? Savor it. Own it. *Enjoy* it!"

Newton swayed unsteadily.

Jenny leaned across to me. "I think Mr. Grunt is a bully," she whispered.

At that moment a big yellow banana came dancing across the field toward us.

Mr. Grunt turned away from the winners' podium and stared.

"What the heck is that?" he said.

Chapter 18

Let's go bananas!

"Looks like Mr. Brainfright has come to cheer us on," I said to Jenny.

"I feel better already," said Jenny, immediately brightening.

Mr. Brainfright finished his entrance with a spectacular series of midair somersaults and ended up on the ground in a split.

Mr. Grunt just stood.

And stared.

I'd never seen him so lost for words.

Mr. Brainfright then jumped to his feet and began a cheerleading chant. "B-A-N-A-N-A-S! Let's go bananas!" He moved around us, encouraging us to join him. We remembered the fun of yesterday and immediately joined in.

"B-A-N-A-N-A-S! Let's go bananas!" we chanted. "B-A-N-A-N-A-S! Let's go bananas!"

It took Mr. Grunt a few minutes to fully understand what was going on.

And when he did, he wasn't happy.

In fact, it looked like he really *was* going to go bananas. "Stop this nonsense right now!" he yelled at us. Then he turned to Mr. Brainfright. "What's the meaning of this interruption to my class?"

Mr. Brainfright took the banana head off. "It's not an interruption," he said. "I'm the new Northwest Southeast Central School mascot. I'm here to bring the team good luck and inspire them to greatness."

"You'll inspire me to kick you from here to the locker rooms if you don't clear off!" snarled Mr. Grunt.

"Be reasonable, Mr. Grunt," said Mr. Brainfright, "I was training all last night for this."

"And I've been training all my *life* for this," said Mr. Grunt, striding over to Mr. Brainfright and getting ready to make good on his threat.

Jenny jumped to her feet. "No!" she cried. "Leave him alone, Mr. Grunt. We need him."

"We need a giant banana?" said Mr. Grunt. "Don't be stupid!"

"It's not stupid!" said Mr. Brainfright. "All sports teams have a mascot. The Northwest soccer team has a grizzly bear mascot. The Northwest hockey team has an eagle. And the Northwest All-Stars basketball team has a giant chicken."

At the mention of the Northwest All-Stars, Mr. Grunt softened and nodded. "Hmm," he said, stroking his chin, "that's true . . ."

"Even Northwest West Academy has a mascot," said Gretel. "Mr. Constrictor's dog, Chomp."

"All right, all right," said Mr. Grunt. "But a giant *banana* is simply ridiculous."

"*Nothing* strikes fear into your opponent's heart like a giant banana," said Mr. Brainfright. "Besides, it's certainly no more ridiculous than a giant chicken!"

Mr. Grunt turned on him. "I won't stand for anybody saying anything against the Northwest All-Stars! They are one of the world's greatest basketball teams! And I could have been their greatest coach ever. If only . . ."

At that moment I noticed Newton still standing on the winner's block, looking very white and unsteady on his feet.

"Mr. Grunt," I said, but Mr. Grunt was staring into space, saying, "If only . . . if only . . ."

"Mr. *Grunt*!" I said, louder this time.

But it was too late. Newton swayed violently and fell forward, off the podium and onto the ground. He sat up, looking dazed.

Jenny went to help him.

The thud of Newton hitting the ground snapped Mr. Grunt out of his daydream. He looked up. "Oh, for goodness sake," he said with his hands on his hips. "Newton Hooton, you are wasting my — and everybody's — time." Then he looked at Mr. Brainfright. "And so are you."

"That's not how Principal Greenbeard sees it," said Mr. Brainfright. "He thinks a banana mascot is a great idea, and he has already given his permission for me to perform on the day."

Mr. Grunt went red with anger. "Oh, did he?" he said. "Well, you DO NOT have permission to interrupt my class with your bizarre antics!"

"I'm sorry you feel that way, Mr. Grunt," said Mr. Brainfright. "But as a fellow teacher I completely respect your right to teach your classes as you see fit. But if you ever need me — "

"Thank you very much," said Mr. Grunt sarcastically, "but if I ever get so desperate that I need to call on you to help me I'll . . . I'll . . . well, I'll NEVER get THAT desperate! Good-bye . . . and good riddance!"

Mr. Brainfright shrugged. "Suit yourself, Mr. Grunt," he said sadly. He put the banana head on and trudged slowly back across the field.

He was down, but not out.

Not by a long shot.

Chapter 19

Just another normal gym class

The rest of our gym class was pretty much business as usual, despite Mr. Brainfright's efforts to inspire us to greatness.

Jack was given another fifty laps for attempting to mount the winners' podium by bunny-hopping his way up to the top. I was given fifty laps for laughing at Jack's attempt at mounting the winners' podium by bunny-hopping up to the top.

Later, during relay practice, Jenny stopped to help the other team when one of their runners dropped her baton and ended up causing an eight-student pileup.

Gretel dropped a shot put on her toes.

Grant snapped a pole-vaulting pole in half.

Clive threw a javelin at Penny's and Gina's imaginary horses and made them cry. (Penny and Gina, that is, not the horses.)

The class ended with Mr. Grunt losing his temper and giving *everybody* fifty laps. All except for Gretel, who had to go and visit Mrs. Bandaid, and came back wearing ten Band-Aids — two on each toe.

Chapter 20

Egg attack!

The next morning we all limped into the school yard in varying degrees of pain. My legs were really hurting from the laps, Jenny had a big bruise on her arm where Clive had fallen on her, and Gretel was on crutches.

"What are we going to do?" said Jenny. "Things are worse than ever!"

"Not as bad as they're about to get!" said Newton, his eyes wide with fear.

"What are you talking about?" said Jenny. "How could things possibly get worse?"

Jenny got her answer in the form of an egg thrown from the window of the Northwest West Academy bus, which seemed to have appeared out of thin air.

The egg hit Jenny's shoulder and splashed its sticky contents all over her dress.

"Good morning, losers!" yelled Troy Gurgling, who was hanging out of the window of the bus, his hands full of eggs. "Wakey, wakey!"

"Egg attack!" Jack yelled. "Run!"

But we were all either too sore or too injured to run, and it was too late, anyway.

The egg that hit Jenny was followed by five more — one for each of us and a bonus second egg for her.

It wasn't fair.

If there was one person in the school who didn't deserve to be hit by one egg — much less two — it was Jenny Friendly. Jenny was the kind of person who spent her whole day thinking about — and looking out for — other people. There wasn't a nicer, more thoughtful person in the whole school, but Northwest West Academy didn't care about that. That's how bad they were. Jenny was standing there, covered in thick, clear, dripping egg-goo, just like the rest of us.

As I wiped egg yolk out of my eyes and watched the smoke-belching bus tear off down the road, I swore revenge.

I didn't know how I was going to get it — I just knew that I would.

I was going to make Northwest West Academy sorry they'd thrown eggs at Jenny Friendly.

I was going to make Northwest West Academy sorry that they had ever been born.

Or my name wasn't Henry McThrottle.

Which it was . . . so it was *definitely* going to happen.

I picked up my bag as well as Jenny's. "Come on," I said to everyone. "Let's go in and get cleaned up."

But before we could leave, Fred and Clive appeared.

"What a bunch of losers you all are!" guffawed Fred.

"Good one, Fred," said Clive.

"We're not losers," I said.

"My mistake," said Fred. "You're a bunch of loser omelets! That's what you are!"

Chapter 21

The Brainfright Program for Sporting Excellence

We went inside the classroom, limping and egg-splattered.

"I'll get the Super Dryer 3000!" said Grant, jumping up and heading toward his locker.

"NO!" we all said at once, imagining ourselves covered in fried eggs.

When Mr. Brainfright entered the room at that moment, he stopped and stared at us. "What happened to you?" he asked.

We told him about Northwest West Academy's latest cowardly attack. And then about what had happened in the rest of our gym class the previous afternoon after he'd been sent packing by Mr. Grunt.

"I wish Mr. Grunt would let you stay and cheer us on," said Jenny. "I'm sure we'd be better if you were there."

"Probably not, though," said Jack. "Let's face it. We're just no good at sports. We couldn't even dodge a few eggs."

"That's not true," said Mr. Brainfright. "Everybody has ability — even you, 5B. You just don't realize it yet . . . and until you realize it, you can't develop it!"

"What do you mean?" said Jenny.

"A mascot is an important spirit-lifter, to be sure, but so is belief in your own abilities. . . . I think it's time to put you all on the Brainfright Program for Sporting Excellence."

"Don't tell me we have to go back outside," whined Newton.

"I'm still tired from yesterday," said Penny.

"I'm covered in egg," said Jack.

"Relax," said Mr. Brainfright, chuckling. "We don't need to go outside. The latest research shows that sporting success has much more to do with the mind than anybody ever suspected. In fact, it's possible that you could actually achieve more sitting here at your desks than you ever could on a field."

"I find that hard to believe," said David.

"Me too," said Jenny. "My mother says that practice makes perfect."

"And she's right," said Mr. Brainfright. "But a recent study suggests that practicing a skill *in your mind* can be just as effective — if not more so — than actually practicing it with your body."

"But how?" said Jenny.

"Well," said Mr. Brainfright, "in this study, they tested two groups of basketball players. One group practiced by playing basketball for half an hour every day. The other group practiced by *imagining* that they were playing basketball for half an hour every day. After a month, the first group showed a definite improvement in their basketball skills, as you would expect. But what was *not* expected was that the second group, who had been doing imaginary practice, actually improved *more*! The researchers conducting the study had no choice but to conclude that the power of the mind is greater than the power of the body."

"But we're not playing basketball against Northwest West Academy," said Clive. "It's a track-and-field competition!"

"Same difference," said Mr. Brainfright. "It doesn't matter what the sport is — you're using the same brain."

"Oh, that's going to be hard for Clive, then," said Jack. "Seeing as he doesn't have one."

"I'm telling my brother you said that," said Clive.

"Actually, Clive," said Jack, "it was your brother who told me that you didn't have a brain in the first place."

Clive looked confused.

"That's enough of that," said Mr. Brainfright. "There are more powerful uses for our brains than using them to accuse each other of not having them."

"It's the truth!" said Jack. "A recent study of the inside of Clive's head showed that it was completely empty."

"That's a lie!" said Clive.

"Clive! Jack!" said Mr. Brainfright. "Come now. We don't have time for this. The competition is on Friday. If Northwest Southeast Central is to have a serious chance at winning we need to get started right away. Everybody sit up straight and close your eyes."

Chapter 22

Visualization

We sat up straight and closed our eyes.

Mr. Brainfright started speaking in a very low, soothing voice. "Imagine that you are on the running track. You are crouched at the starting line. You can feel the spongy surface of the running track through the soles of your running shoes. Your fingers are touching the ground lightly. Your leg muscles are coiled like powerful springs. Electricity is shooting through your body. You can hear the roar of the crowd. You can smell your opponents' sweat."

"Eww!" said Jenny.

"You can feel the sun on the back of your neck — "

"Ouch! It's burning," said Newton.

"No, it isn't," said Mr. Brainfright in his soothing voice, "because you applied sunscreen just before you left the locker rooms."

"What strength was it?" said Newton. "I don't think it's working."

"Thirty SPF," said Mr. Brainfright.

"I need *fifty* SPF," said Newton. "I have very sensitive skin."

"Fifty it is then," said Mr. Brainfright, sighing.

"Thanks," said Newton.

"The starter's pistol fires," said Mr. Brainfright. "You take off. You run like the wind. Your legs are pumping like pistons. Your arms are pumping like . . . um . . . er . . . pistons. You look around you. Your competitors are a long way behind. You feel the ribbon break against your chest. You mount the winners' podium — "

"Can I just stand on the second-place block, please?" asked Newton.

"No, it's the winner's block for you, Newton," said Mr. Brainfright. "You won the race!"

"But it's too high on the first block," said Newton.

"I'm sorry, Newton," said Mr. Brainfright, "but in the Brainfright Program for Sporting Excellence, you are a winner, and winners have excellent balance and nerves of steel. Trust me."

"I'll give it a try," Newton said.

"Good," Mr. Brainfright continued. "So — now that we have that straight — you mount the winners' podium and climb to the highest block."

"I'm doing it!" said Newton excitedly. "I'm *actually* doing it."

"Good for you, Newton," said Mr. Brainfright. "Good for all of you. You are *all* standing on the highest block."

"Isn't it a bit dangerous for us *all* to be standing on the same block?" Fiona questioned.

"No," said Mr. Brainfright. "You are each standing on your *own* winners' podium."

"What, did *everyone* win the race?" asked David. "Did we all come in first?"

"Yes!" said Mr. Brainfright. "There are no losers in the Brainfright Program for Sporting Excellence. You are all winners. Each and every one of you. You bow your head and feel the weight of the gold medal as it is placed around your neck. You turn to the crowd and raise your right fist in the air. The crowd roars. You feel amazing, powerful. There is no one you can't beat."

"Except for Northwest West Academy," said Jack.

"No, Jack," said Mr. Brainfright patiently. "*Even* Northwest West Academy."

Mr. Brainfright took us through all the events.

For the hurdles, he had us imagine we were horses running in the annual Northwest steeplechase. We flew over those jumps like Thoroughbreds, fast and strong and sure of foot.

We fired shot puts from our hands as if we were long-range cannons.

We threw discuses across the entire length of the field as if they were as light as Frisbees.

We hurled javelins as if we were primeval hunters relying on our accuracy and skill for our very lives.

We pole-vaulted as if we were desperate prisoners making a last-ditch attempt to scale the walls of Alcatraz.

We ran long-distance races as if we were being chased by wild, man-eating animals.

We even did the triple jump as if the ground beneath us was covered in red-hot lava.

And we won!

We won event after event.

We were unstoppable!

Chapter 23

Bananas

For the next two days we continued to do the Brainfright Program for Sporting Excellence in the morning, after lunch, and just before school finished for the day.

And when we weren't doing visualizations, we were learning about bananas.

Now, we knew Mr. Brainfright really liked bananas. After all, he did once spend a whole lesson teaching us how to eat a banana. But it was starting to get ridiculous. Since he'd started wearing the banana suit, *all* our lessons were about bananas.

Mr. Brainfright was standing at the front of the classroom in his banana suit.

"Well, 5B," he said. "I think it's time we brushed up on some more banana facts. Did you know that bananas grow in clusters called 'hands,' and that each banana is called a 'finger'?"

We all shook our heads — except for Fiona. "I did," she said.

"Very good, Fiona," said Mr. Brainfright. "But did

you know that bananas are grown in at least one hundred and seven countries?"

Fiona's eyes opened wide. "No, I didn't know that!" she said, making a note.

Mr. Brainfright continued, "And did you know that there's a variety of banana — called the lady finger banana — that you don't eat when it's yellow, but wait until it's gone black?"

I groaned and put my head down on my desk.

"What's the matter, Henry?" said Mr. Brainfright.

"Can we *please* learn about something other than bananas?" I pleaded.

Mr. Brainfright frowned, and then smiled. "Of course," he said. "What did you have in mind? Would you like to do some math?"

"Yes!" I said, which just goes to show how desperate I was.

"All right, then," he said, "if I had two regular bananas in this hand and three sugar bananas in this hand, how many bananas would I have altogether?"

"That's not math," I said. "That's just more about bananas!"

"I'm sorry," said Mr. Brainfright, looking a little hurt. "It's just that bananas are *so* interesting. But maybe you have a point, Henry. Perhaps I have been too narrow in my teaching of late. There is more to learn about than just bananas. For example, there are also plantains, which are very closely related to bananas. . . ."

And on he went.

And on.

And on.

And on.

Chapter 24

Mr. Brainfright's top ten facts about bananas

1. Bananas grow in bunches called "hands." Each banana in a hand is called a "finger," and the trees they grow on are called "palms."
2. Bananas can cure warts.
3. Bananas are the fruit most likely to be used to make a banana cake.
4. Their name is the most fun of all fruit names to spell aloud.
5. Bananas are the leading cause of bride-related injuries, as documented in the song, "Here comes the bride, all dressed in white, slipped on a banana peel, and went for a ride!"
6. Bananas are very peaceful. They are definitely the quietest of all fruits.
7. Bananas are the fruit most likely to be left in the bottom of a school bag.
8. Bananas are the fruit most likely to be used to imitate a telephone.
9. Bananas feature in more jokes than any other fruit. For example:

Person A: There's a banana in your ear.

Person B: What?

Person A: I said, *"There's a banana in your ear."*

Person B: Pardon?

Person A: THERE'S A BANANA IN YOUR EAR!!!

Person B: Look, I'm sorry I can't hear you because, you see, I have a banana in my ear.

10. Bananas were voted Most Popular Fruit in a recent *Monkey's Monthly Magazine* readers' poll.

Chapter 25

Art class

Things got even worse after that.

Mr. Brainfright started wearing the banana suit all the time.

At first he'd just worn it when he was doing visualizations, but now he kept it on all day.

And he was still teaching us about bananas.

We learned about the history of bananas.

We did addition with bananas.

We read stories about bananas.

We acted like bananas.

By the time it got to Wednesday morning, we couldn't wait for art class. Mrs. Rainbow never talked about bananas at all.

So you can imagine our surprise — and disappointment — when we arrived at the art room, and a giant banana wearing an art smock greeted us at the door.

"Hello, children!" said Mr. Brainfright cheerfully.

"Mr. Brainfright?" I said, taken aback. "What are you doing here?"

"Well," said Mr. Brainfright, "Mrs. Rainbow is ill, and she asked me if I would step in and teach the class for her today."

Jack, Jenny, Gretel, Newton, and I looked at one another with our mouths open.

"Mr. Brainfright," said Jack, "I don't want to be rude, but will this class be about bananas?"

"Of course not," said Mr. Brainfright. "This is art class!"

"And you won't make us *draw* bananas?" said Gretel.

"No drawing bananas," said Mr. Brainfright. "I promise . . . unless you *want* to, of course."

"No!" said Gretel quickly.

"And we won't be *making* bananas out of papier-mâché, clay, or Popsicle sticks?" said Jenny.

"I promise you faithfully that we will do none of these things," said Mr. Brainfright.

It seemed too good to be true, but a promise was a promise. We relaxed a little.

"So what are we going to do then?" said Jack.

"Well," said Mr. Brainfright, "I thought today we would concentrate on colors! Is that all right with you?"

We nodded. And relaxed even more.

"Who can tell me how many colors there are in a rainbow?" asked Mr. Brainfright.

Fiona's hand shot up. "Oh, that's easy!" she said. "Seven! Red, orange, yellow, green, blue, indigo, and violet."

"Very good, Fiona," said Mr. Brainfright. "And who can tell me which is the best color of them all?"

Fiona's hand was still up. "Do you mean which color is our favorite?" she said.

"No," said Mr. Brainfright. "I mean which color is the *best*."

Then Fiona did a strange thing.

She put her hand down.

Astonishing as it seemed, she didn't know the answer!

"Nobody knows?" said Mr. Brainfright. "Nobody? Why, it's *yellow* of course!"

"Uh-oh," Jack said under his breath.

"Yellow?" said Fiona. "Why yellow?"

"Isn't it obvious?" said Mr. Brainfright. "Yellow is wonderful! It's the color of the sun! And the color of daisies! It's the color of cheerfulness and it's also the color used on warning signs — so yellow helps keep us safe! It's the color of all of the most precious things in the world: of amber . . . and gold . . . and . . ."

"*Bananas*, by any chance?" asked Jack, rolling his eyes.

"Yes!" boomed Mr. Brainfright. "Bananas! There's no doubt about it, yellow is definitely the best color there is!"

"I'm not so sure about that," said Fiona. "What about green? Green is good, too. It's the color of grass, trees, and vegetables . . . vegetables are very good for you, you know."

"Vegetables are overrated," snapped Mr. Brainfright. "They certainly aren't as good as bananas! Besides, where would vegetables be without the sun — which, may I remind you, is *yellow!*"

Jack and I exchanged a surprised look. We'd never seen Mr. Brainfright like this before. He didn't seem like the Mr. Brainfright we knew.

"But that's ridiculous!" said Fiona.

"Don't argue with me!" said Mr. Brainfright. "Yellow is the best color, and that's all there is to it. And there's not just yellow-yellow, either. There are more than thirty-two different shades of yellow! Gold, amber, golden-yellow, golden-amber, lemon, mustard, saffron — "

"Yes, Mr. Brainfright," said Jack, attempting to pacify him. "You're definitely right. . . . We get the point."

But Mr. Brainfright was not to be stopped. He droned on and on, apparently intent on naming every single one of yellow's thirty-two shades. "Corn, flax, school-bus yellow, banana — "

"Will we be tested on this?" asked Fiona, interrupting him.

"You bet you will!" said Mr. Brainfright. "In fact, we'll have a test right now!"

"But you can't test us right away!" Fiona protested. "You didn't warn us beforehand!"

"Yeah," complained Clive. "It's not fair. I'm going to tell my brother!"

"Warning! Warning!" said Mr. Brainfright sarcastically. "In one second, there will be a test." He paused. "There! Consider yourselves warned! The test begins now. What frequency of the color chart does yellow occupy — 90 hertz, 100 hertz, 400 hertz, or 500 hertz?"

Everybody in the class looked at one another. How were *we* supposed to know that? How was *anyone* supposed to know that?

Even Fiona and David were looking confused.

Mr. Brainfright never tested us. In fact, he hated tests. Maybe even more than we did.

Something was wrong.

Something was seriously, definitely, terribly wrong.

Chapter 26

The great banana milk mystery

After art class finally finished, we had lunch. Then we trudged slowly back into the classroom.

We didn't mind the visualizations, but we were dreading more banana lessons.

Our first sight of Mr. Brainfright was not promising.

He was standing at the front of the room, in full banana suit, holding a container of banana-flavored milk in his hand.

"Oh, no," I whispered to Jack. "I can't take any more!"

"Me neither," said Jack. "Let's make a run for it! The window's wide open!"

"Good idea," I said. "Let's go!"

We were about to run across the room and jump out the window when Mr. Brainfright yelled at us.

"Where do you think you're going?" he said. "Sit down!"

Jack and I looked at each other, undecided about what to do.

But Mr. Brainfright decided it for us. "Now!" he said sharply.

There was an edge to Mr. Brainfright's voice that we'd never heard before. He was mad. And not just banana-mad, either — he was mad-mad.

"All right, 5B," said Mr. Brainfright when we were all sitting down. He held up the container of milk. "I presume you know what this is?"

Fiona's hand shot up. "It's a five-ounce container of flavored milk, sir," she said.

"That's right, Fiona," said Mr. Brainfright. "And can anyone tell me what flavor it is?"

For once I knew the answer to one of his questions, but I didn't dare answer it. Nobody did. Except for Fiona, who could never resist an opportunity to show off her knowledge.

"Banana-flavored, sir!" she said.

Mr. Brainfright nodded. "That's right," he said, sadly shaking his head. "Banana. Can you believe it?"

"Yes," said Fiona, not even bothering to put up her hand anymore. "I believe banana is the third most popular flavor in the cafeteria, after chocolate and strawberry."

"Well, it's wrong!" shouted Mr. Brainfright. "Do you hear me? It's completely against the natural order of things!"

Fiona just looked at him, stunned.

She didn't speak.

She couldn't speak.

None of us could.

And I'll bet you wouldn't be able to, either, if a giant banana was standing over you, shouting and waving an empty carton of banana-flavored milk in your face.

"A banana DIED to make this milk!" said Mr. Brainfright, stalking up and down in between the rows of our desks, waving the carton in each of our faces. "And drinking it makes you no better than a murderer!"

I glanced at Jenny, Gretel, Jack, and Newton.

None of us knew what to make of this latest development.

It didn't make sense. After all, it was Mr. Brainfright who, in one of his very first classes, had taught us how to eat, and really *taste*, a banana.

Now here he was accusing us of being murderers if we so much as dared to drink banana-flavored milk.

As strange and unlikely as it seemed, Mr. Brainfright had gone from appreciating bananas, and dressing up as a banana to . . . well, there's no other way to put it . . . to *thinking* like a banana.

Chapter 27

Mascot madness

On Wednesday morning, we were standing outside the library listening to Mr. Shush giving us his usual warning about all the things that we were not to do once we got inside the library.

"And furthermore," he said, taking a deep breath, "there is to be no *juggling* of the books, no using the books as *Frisbees*, and definitely no *kicking* the books. . . ."

Jack shook his head. "No *kicking* the books?" he muttered. "What does he think we are? Wild animals?"

"Yes," said Mr. Shush, who had exceptionally good hearing. "That's *exactly* what I think you are. If it were up to me, I wouldn't allow students in the library at all."

"Can we go in now?" said David.

"Yes, I suppose so," said Mr. Shush, "if you must. But make sure you each wipe your feet properly. I don't want any mud in the library, and certainly no mud on any of the books!"

"You already told us that, Mr. Shush," said Gretel as she wiped her feet and went inside.

"Shush!" said Mr. Shush. "You're inside a *library* now."

Once we were inside and safely seated at the study tables, we did quite well at resisting the temptation to juggle, Frisbee, kick, or smear mud all over the books. But we didn't do so well at not talking and, as usual, poor Mr. Shush was run off his feet dashing from table to table shushing people.

The only person who was actually *reading* a book was Fiona. She had her head down and was studying an enormous medical textbook. We knew the book well, as we'd spent many hours combing it for photographs of particularly gruesome medical conditions.

"Any good pictures, Fiona?" said Jack.

"Don't show them!" said Newton, who was terrified of photographs of gruesome medical conditions. He was probably more terrified of the photographs than the medical conditions themselves. To tell you the truth, we all were — but that didn't stop us from looking at them.

"Don't worry, Newton," said Fiona, finally raising her head. "I haven't found any photographs, but I've found some *very* interesting information. I think I know what's wrong with Mr. Brainfright!"

"What is it?" asked Jenny.

80

"He's got *mascot madness*," said Fiona.

"Mascot madness?" said Newton, turning white. "That sounds scary!"

"It's nothing to be scared of, Newton," said Fiona. "But it *is* serious. Mascot madness is a medical term for a rare but well-documented condition in which the wearer of a mascot costume begins to identify completely with that costume. They forget who they are and come to think of the character they are playing as their true identity."

"Can we have that again, but in English this time?" said Jack.

"Simply stated," said Fiona, "Mr. Brainfright is no longer himself. He thinks he is a banana."

"That's the stupidest thing I've ever heard!" said Gretel.

"No, it's not," said Fiona, her finger on the book. "Listen to this: 'The effects of mascot madness are very difficult to categorize. They manifest differently in each individual case. For example, Mr. Simmons of Central City, who served as a gorilla mascot for the Central City Ping-Pong team, came to identify with his suit so completely that he believed he really *was* a gorilla.'"

"Did he recover?" said Jenny.

"No," said Fiona, shaking her head. She looked back at the book. "He is now a popular tourist attraction in the gorilla enclosure of the Northwest

Zoo. And then there's Mrs. Beek of Northwest West West West, who was an eagle mascot for the Northwest West West West volleyball team. She was cured of her madness after jumping out of a tree in an attempt to fly. It is believed that the shock of the fall snapped her out of it. . . ."

"That's terrible!" said Jenny. "That poor woman!"

"At least she got better," I pointed out.

"Yes," said Fiona solemnly. "But it gets worse. There's the tragic case of Mr. White of Central City Central, who, a mere seven weeks after wearing a shark mascot costume for less than an hour each day, went to his local swimming pool, where he attacked several swimmers and . . ." Fiona shut the book. "I can't read any more," she said. "It's too awful!"

Jack grabbed the book and started flipping through it, obviously in search of the gruesome details. "Are there any pictures?" he asked.

"Shush!" said Mr. Shush. "This is a library, not a yelling competition!"

"I *wasn't* yelling," whispered Jack.

"YES, YOU WERE!" yelled Mr. Shush.

"Shush, Mr. Shush!" whispered Jack. "This is a library, not a yelling competition."

"My point exactly!" said Mr. Shush, walking away.

"Does it say anything in there about how to cure mascot madness?" asked Jenny.

"Not really," said Fiona. "So little is known about the condition that it's hard to say, but it appears that some people can be snapped out of it by a shock. Others, however — like that poor gorilla man — never come out of it."

"Well, we should try shocking Mr. Brainfright," I said. "I want the old Mr. Brainfright back. He's not as much fun as a banana as he was as a human being."

"I agree, Henry," said Gretel, "but I think we should wait until *after* the track-and-field competition. It's more important that he remains a banana . . . at least until tomorrow afternoon."

"But he's not a banana!" said Jenny. "He's a *human being!*"

"I know that, and you know that," said Fiona, "but *he* doesn't know that. He thinks he's a banana. And in a very real sense he is — a very *good* banana — and one that could be crucial to our chances of winning on Friday."

There was a pause.

Fiona looked at us.

We looked at Fiona.

Finally, Jenny spoke. "Are you suggesting that we . . . do nothing?"

Fiona shook her head. "Not exactly. I certainly think we should do *something* . . . just not until after Friday."

Jenny frowned. "But . . ."

83

"Think about it, Jenny," said Gretel. "If we cure him now, he might not be such an effective mascot on Friday and, let's face it, we need all the help we can get."

"I want to win the games as much as everybody else does," said Jenny, "but not at Mr. Brainfright's expense!"

"But it's not like Mr. Brainfright is unhappy, Jenny," I said. "I mean, there isn't anything actually *wrong* with him."

"Henry," said Jenny, "there's something wrong with *you* if you can't see the problem here. He thinks he's a *banana!*"

"I know that!" I said. "All I'm saying is let's not do anything that we might regret. We can't let Northwest West Academy walk all over us again. Milk! Eggs! What's next? We can't continue living in fear!"

"Yeah," said Jack, looking up from the big medical book. "It's not hurting anyone to let him think he's a banana for another day or two. After all, it's not as if he's about to jump into a swimming pool and start chewing on people's legs."

"Jack's right," said Fiona. "The chances of being attacked by a banana are statistically very low . . . and even if you were, you could just squash it with your foot."

"Really?" said Newton.

"Really!" said Fiona in a reassuring voice.

84

I could have told Fiona a few things about exactly how dangerous that banana suit was, but I didn't want to upset Newton or endanger our best-ever chance of beating Northwest West Academy.

Jenny shook her head. "I think you're all being really mean," she said.

"How about we take a vote on it?" said Fiona. "That's the fair way to decide. All in favor of doing nothing, put up your hands."

Fiona put up her hand.

I put up my hand.

Jack put up his hand.

Gretel put up her hand.

Newton looked worried, and then put up his hand.

Jenny picked up her books, stood up, and went and sat at another table.

Chapter 28

Sorry

The next morning I was in the school yard, waiting for Jenny to arrive. After our library session yesterday she had refused to talk to any of the gang for the rest of the day.

As she came in the gate, she saw me, turned away, and hurried off in the other direction.

"Jenny," I called after her, "wait! I want to talk to you!"

She kept on walking — only faster.

I ran after her and put my hand on her shoulder. She stopped.

"What do you want, Henry?" she asked.

"I just wanted to apologize," I said. "I know how you feel about Mr. Brainfright."

"Do you?" she said. "Then why didn't you vote to try to help him?"

"Because there are other issues here," I said.

"What?" said Jenny impatiently. "That you need somebody dancing around in a banana costume to make you believe in yourself?"

"No," I said. "But . . ."

86

Suddenly, Newton, Jack, and Gretel yelled at us from the other side of the yard. "Henry! Jenny! Watch out! They're coming!"

We didn't have to ask who they meant.

We could already smell the choking fumes and hear the horn of the bus as it roared toward the school.

"Don't anybody move!" said Jenny.

"Are you crazy?" I said.

"No," she said, walking toward the front of the school. "Come with me!"

"Jenny?" I said, wondering if mascot madness was contagious. "Are you feeling all right?"

"Never better!" she said. "Come on!"

Chapter 29

Tomato attack

Jenny was standing by the fence, right beside the road.

And the Northwest West Academy bus was coming!

My instinct was to run . . . but I couldn't. Not with Jenny out there. I reluctantly ran after her.

The bus was loud now. We could hear the Northwest West students yelling at us. They were mostly unintelligible, but the word "LOSERS" was loud and clear.

I looked around me.

Jenny and I were flanked by Newton, Gretel, and Jack. The rest of the students had ducked for cover.

Troy Gurgling leaned out of the bus window and yelled, "Fire!"

Red objects flew out of the bus windows.

A rotten-tomato attack!

I wanted to run, but I resisted the temptation and then, to my utter surprise, I flung out my arms and caught a tomato in each hand. I wasn't the only one. Jack, Jenny, Gretel, and Newton each caught a couple as well.

There was a moment where everything seemed to stop.

The yelling from the bus stopped.

We stopped.

"Let's go!" yelled Jenny.

We went.

We sprinted out the school gate, up the road, and after the bus.

The surprised faces of Troy Gurgling and other Northwest West Academy students were pressed against the back window of the bus. But, for a change, instead of yelling at us about what losers we were, they were yelling at their bus driver to drive faster.

Their surprise was only exceeded by ours.

We could hardly believe how effortlessly we were gaining on the bus. Running had always seemed hard work, but now it was as easy as if we were being blown along by the wind.

When we got close to the bus, Jenny gave the command to launch our tomatoes.

"Fire!" she shouted.

We fired — the first wave from our right hands, the second wave from our left.

The back window of the Northwest West Academy bus was covered in the red splodge of ten rotten tomatoes.

"See you tomorrow!" yelled Jack, as we slowed down and watched the bus speed away.

"That was fun!" said Newton, walking straighter than I'd ever seen him.

I nodded. "You can say that again."

I looked across at Jenny. "You were right," I said. "We can do it on our own, banana or no."

She just smiled.

Chapter 30

Mr. Grunt's program

As we walked back into the school yard, the rest of the Northwest Southeast Central School students gave us a rousing cheer.

"Well, I'll be darned," said Mr. Grunt. "Way to go, kids! Looks like my cutting-edge training is finally paying off. Took a few years, but it's definitely working."

We looked at each other and grinned.

We knew the truth.

It was nothing to do with Mr. Grunt's training. It was Mr. Brainfright's Program for Sporting Excellence that was finally paying off.

Mr. Grunt was the happiest I've ever seen him. "I knew, of course, that prolonged exposure to an expert athlete like myself would have to affect your performance sooner or later. After all, how could you watch me for all this time and not learn anything? It's ridiculous!"

"It's not watching you that's made us better," said Jack, unable to endure Mr. Grunt's boasting a moment longer. "It's Mr. Brainfright."

"You think having a banana mascot has made you better at sports?" Mr. Grunt snorted.

"Not *just* the mascotting," said Gretel. "It's the visualizations."

"What?!" spat Mr. Grunt.

"We've been training in our minds," said Fiona.

"That's preposterous," said Mr. Grunt. "The mind has nothing to do with sports. And I should know!" He leaned down and yelled into Fiona's face. "NO PAIN, NO GAIN."

"Not necessarily," said Fiona, stepping back. "You should never underestimate the power of the mind."

"So it's Brainfright who's been filling your heads with this nonsense, is it?" snarled Mr. Grunt. "I should have known."

"Yes," said Jenny enthusiastically. "He's put us on the Brainfright Program for Sporting Excellence."

"Well, I'll teach him to interfere," barked Mr. Grunt. "I'm going to introduce him to a little program of my own. It's called the Grunt Program for Minding Your Own Business."

"Is that a threat?" said David.

"No!" said Mr. Grunt. "It's a promise!"

Chapter 31

A visit from Mr. Grunt

When we arrived at our classroom, Mr. Brainfright was still in his banana suit, but he appeared to be a little less crazy than he had been for the last few days.

"I owe you all an apology," he said. "I think I may have gotten a bit carried away and crossed the line from banana mascot to banana bore."

Jenny and I looked at each other.

This was definitely a positive sign.

Perhaps Mr. Brainfright wasn't suffering from mascot madness after all. Maybe there was nothing to worry about.

"I guess I'm just so excited about tomorrow," he said. "I really want to do a good job and be the best mascot I can be. I don't want to let you down."

"Just relax," I said. "You're going to be great. We all are!"

The class murmured its assent.

"Give me a B!" yelled Mr. Brainfright.

We were about to give Mr. Brainfright a "B" when the door flew open and Mr. Grunt burst in. He always looked ugly, but this time he was looking even uglier than usual.

"I'll give you a 'B,' all right!" he barked at Mr. Brainfright. "And I'll give you a good kick on the B-hind as well!"

"Mr. Grunt!" said Mr. Brainfright. "What a lovely surprise!"

"Don't you 'Mr. Grunt what a lovely surprise' me!" said Mr. Grunt. "I've got a bone to pick with you, Brainfright!"

"That's going to be a little difficult, I'm afraid!" said Mr. Brainfright. "You see, bananas don't have any bones."

Mr. Grunt stared blankly at Mr. Brainfright for a moment. Then he shook his head and continued. "Listen to me, Brainfright," he said. "It might not mean much to you, since you haven't been at this school for very long, but every year we have a very important sports competition. As the gym teacher, I spend all year preparing my students for this event with a highly planned combination of hard training and cutting-edge coaching techniques, and I do *not* appreciate someone like you coming in and messing everything up at the last minute."

"But I haven't been messing everything up!" said Mr. Brainfright. "I've been helping!"

"Is that what you call it?" said Mr. Grunt. "Dressing up in a ridiculous banana suit and messing with the

94

heads of our students? Well, I don't call that help. I call that interference!"

Mr. Brainfright smiled and shook his head. "My methods are a little . . . uh . . . unconventional, it's true . . . but they are based on sound scientific principles. Mascots have been used throughout history to bring good luck to sports teams . . . and the latest mind-body research is *very* exciting. . . ."

"Stop right there, Brainfright," said Mr. Grunt. "I'll tell you what would be exciting. It would be exciting if you would spare me this nonsense and let me get on with the business of preparing the Northwest Southeast Central students for the big day tomorrow."

"Why, certainly," said Mr. Brainfright. "But nobody has all the answers — we can all use a little help."

"What's that supposed to mean?" said Mr. Grunt.

"Nothing," said Mr. Brainfright. "Merely that Northwest West Academy has proven a hard team to beat in the past, and your track record is, well, let's say, *less than impressive.* . . ."

Now, one thing to remember when you're dealing with Mr. Grunt is that you should *never* refer to his track record. And if you *do* have to refer to his track record, you should definitely avoid the words "less than impressive." Unfortunately, Mr. Brainfright didn't know this . . . but he was about to find out.

Chapter 32

Grunt versus Brainfright

"Right, that does it!" said Mr. Grunt, curling his large hands into even larger fists and raising them up in front of his face. "I'm not going to stand here and have some crazy banana-brained egghead trample all over my reputation and tell me how to do my job. Put up or shut up, Brainfright!"

Jenny raised her hands to her mouth in horror. "No!" she gasped.

Newton dived underneath his desk.

"I think you'll find that fighting in class is against the school rules," said David, holding up his handbook.

Mr. Grunt snatched the book from David and threw it out the window. "I'll fight WHO I like, WHEN I like, WHERE I like!" he shouted.

"Now, really!" said Mr. Brainfright. "I don't want to fight you, Mr. Grunt."

"Why not?" said Mr. Grunt, bouncing around on his toes, jabbing at Mr. Brainfright's banana head. "Are you yellow?"

"Of course I'm yellow," said Mr. Brainfright, "and proud of it! I'm a banana! You wouldn't hit a piece of fruit, would you?"

"You're not a *piece* of fruit," said Mr. Grunt. "You're a fruitcake! That's what you are!"

And saying that, Mr. Grunt reached out and pulled Mr. Brainfright's head off.

Well, when I say that he pulled Mr. Brainfright's head off, I don't mean that he pulled Mr. Brainfright's *actual* head off — I mean that he pulled Mr. Brainfright's banana-suit head off.

Things happened fast after that.

Mr. Brainfright grabbed for the head.

Mr. Grunt held it up high in the air, out of Mr. Brainfright's reach.

Mr. Brainfright jumped and, as he landed, he accidentally bumped into Mr. Grunt and knocked him sideways.

Mr. Grunt dropped the banana head, but while he tried to regain his balance he stepped on it, slipped, and went skidding across the classroom . . . right out the window!

"Oh, dear," said Mr. Brainfright, picking up his banana head and putting it back on. "I don't think he's going to be very happy about that."

Chapter 33

Grunt versus Spade

Mr. Brainfright was right.

Mr. Grunt was not happy.

We knew this because we could hear him shouting from the flower bed below.

We all rushed to the window.

Mr. Grunt was lying on his back, shaking his fist up at Mr. Brainfright.

"You'll be sorry, Brainfright!" he yelled. "Undoing all my good work with your crazy schemes! I'll get you for this!"

But Mr. Grunt wasn't the only one who was unhappy.

Zooming across the yard toward him was Mr. Spade. And this time he was on his riding mower. He was steering with one hand and waving his pitchfork with the other.

"Get out of my flower bed, Grunt!" he shouted over the noise of the mower's engine. "Get out of my flower bed or I'll turn you into compost!"

Mr. Grunt got to his feet and ran for his life.

Mr. Spade revved his engine and chased after him.

"Come back here, Grunt!" he yelled. "I'm going to . . ."

We couldn't catch the next threat as it was drowned out by the deep throaty roar of Mr. Grunt's Hummer. He'd made it to the parking lot, jumped into his car, and was now escaping at high speed out of the school gates and down the road.

Mr. Spade, however, was not going to give up the chase. He kept right on after Mr. Grunt. He followed him out of the driveway and up the road, making surprising speed.

"That's amazing!" said Grant as they disappeared into the distance. "How can Mr. Spade get so much power out of that tiny motor? Wait till my dad hears about this!"

Mr. Brainfright was dancing and chanting, cheering Mr. Spade on. "Go, Spade, go! Mow! Mow! Mow!"

We all joined in for a few rounds before Mr. Brainfright changed to another cheer. "He wrecked your flower bed! Mow Grunt's head!"

The class started chanting the new cheer enthusiastically. I was doing it, too, till Jenny shook my shoulder roughly. "Henry!" she said. "That's not very nice!"

"It's only Mr. Grunt," I said.

"It doesn't matter who it is," she replied. "It's not nice to mow anyone's head."

"Sorry," I said. "I guess you're right. It's just that Mr. Brainfright is so persuasive."

"Yes, he is," said Jenny, a concerned look on her face. "But I think his madness is getting worse. I'm worried that we'll *never* get the old Mr. Brainfright back."

Chapter 34

Northwest West Academy welcomes us to the stadium . . . NOT!

It was Friday morning.

The big day had finally arrived.

Our class was unlucky enough to have been put on the first bus. We sat in our seats, quiet and miserable. Despite our mascot, our visualizations, and our success in returning Northwest West Academy's tomato attack, we didn't really expect today to be any different than the preceding track-and-field competitions.

At the end of the day, Northwest West Academy would be holding the gold cup high above their heads, while we hung ours in miserable defeat.

The only person who didn't seem to realize this was Mr. Brainfright — and at this point, Mr. Brainfright wasn't even technically a person.

He was a banana.

A big, yellow, dancing banana.

Decked out in his suit, he was dancing up and

down the bus aisle, trying his hardest to lift our spirits.

Our spirits, however, did not exactly lift at the sight of a large group of jeering Northwest West Academy students standing in the parking lot with a banner that read GO HOME, LOSERS!

"That's not very nice!" said Jenny.

"*Northwest West Academy* is not very nice, in case you'd forgotten," I said.

"Let me handle this," said Mr. Brainfright, making his way to the front of the bus. "Let's give them a little taste of *banana power*, shall we?! Open the door, driver! We've got a track-and-field competition to blitz!"

The bus driver, a tired-looking man who'd driven too many busloads of demoralized Northwest Southeast Central students to and from the Northwest Stadium over the years, looked at Mr. Brainfright with great sympathy. He'd seen us get beaten too many times before to believe that a man in a banana suit was going to make any difference.

"It's your funeral, Banana Boy," he said as he shrugged and opened the door of the bus.

"B-A-N-A-N-A-S!" chanted Mr. Brainfright defiantly as he launched himself off the bus.

Now, it *could* have been great.

It could even have been inspiring.

It could have struck fear into the hearts of our opponents.

But it didn't.

Because Mr. Brainfright tripped and fell out of the bus.

He landed on his back, his arms and legs flailing helplessly in the air.

The Northwest West Academy students laughed and applauded.

"Way to go!" yelled Troy Gurgling, looking bigger and uglier than ever.

"Want a hand back onto the bus?" said Troy. "I'd hate to see a nice banana like you get all squashed!"

"Or stomped on!" snickered one of his leering friends, stamping his feet.

"Or mashed up!" sneered another, grinding his fist into his open palm.

"This is no place for bananas," said Troy. "Or for Northwest Southeast Central School losers. Why don't you all just go right back home and save yourselves the trouble of actually competing? We all know who's going to win. Am I right or am I right?"

"Right! Right!" chanted the other Northwest West Academy thugs enthusiastically.

"They're probably right," said Newton in a small voice. "I think we should just go home."

"I think someone should help Mr. Brainfright," said Jenny. She rushed off the bus and helped him to his feet. "You should be ashamed of yourselves," she said to the Northwest West students.

"You're the one who should be ashamed!" said Troy. "You should be ashamed of yourselves for being such losers! We're just trying to save you the disappointment of trying and losing again."

"Thanks for your concern," said Jenny, helping Mr. Brainfright to his feet and brushing dirt off his suit. "But don't worry about us. You should be worrying about yourselves, because this year you've got another thing coming!"

"B-A-N-A-N-A-S!" yelled Mr. Brainfright, punching his fist into the air. "Let's go . . . BANANAS!"

The Northwest West Academy students looked at one another . . . and laughed.

It wasn't exactly a promising start.

And it was about to get even worse.

Chapter 35

Inside the stadium

Although we were all for staying on the bus, Jenny's selfless action in assisting Mr. Brainfright shamed us into getting off.

But things didn't look any more promising when we got inside the stadium.

Instead of a small group of jeering Northwest West Academy students, there was an entire grandstand full of them.

And if you thought GO HOME, LOSERS! wasn't very nice, well, that was positively welcoming compared to the rest of their banners: NORTHWEST SOUTHEAST CENTRAL NINCOMPOOPS!, GREENBEARD'S GUTLESS WONDERS!, and EVERYBODY HATES NORTHWEST SOUTHEAST CENTRAL SCHOOL! are the only ones I can print here because the rest contained words that are banned in our school handbook.

In the middle of the field the Northwest West Academy brass band was playing their tuneless school anthem.

It was hard to make out the actual words, but

there was no doubt about the chorus, which the whole school sang enthusiastically:

Northwest West!
We are the best!
Chuck out the rest!
When put to the test,
we are the best!
Yeah! We are the best
in the whole Northwest!
We're Northwest West
. . . Academy!

"*Academy?*" said Fiona disdainfully. "That doesn't even rhyme."

But worst of all — worse even than their offensive banners, their horrible music, or their poor rhymes — were the scary Mr. Constrictor and Chomp, the even scarier Northwest West Academy mascot.

Although Mr. Constrictor was supposed to be an *ex*–pro wrestler, you would never have known it to look at him. He was still heavily muscled and bald, and his face appeared to be permanently frozen into a scowl. All that was missing was his trademark snakeskin leotard.

Mr. Grunt, on the other hand, was not looking quite so strong.

Arriving on the second bus, he entered the stadium limping, and had what looked like a tire track across his face.

We followed Mr. Grunt to our seats in the stand and sat down.

We had no school band.

We had no banners.

All we had was a dancing banana.

Chapter 36

Banana power!

Mind you, the dancing banana was doing its absolute best to get us all revved up.

Mr. Brainfright was jumping, punching, kicking, spinning on his back, moonwalking, twisting, turning, and chanting with incredible energy. He looked more like a yellow tornado than a banana.

The Northwest West Academy students responded to Mr. Brainfright's efforts with howls of laughter. They pointed, slapped their knees, and pelted him with trash.

"Hey, Banana Boy!" yelled Mr. Constrictor. "We're going to make a smoothie out of you!"

Mr. Brainfright ignored them all and just kept right on dancing.

Even if you thought he did look silly, you had to admit that he had courage.

"I'll show you what we think of bananas around here!" Mr. Constrictor yelled. He produced a banana and tossed it in front of Chomp. The dog leaped upon it and tore it to shreds.

Mr. Brainfright stopped dancing and stared at Chomp.

Chomp bared his teeth and stared back at Mr. Brainfright, strings of foamy drool falling from his jaws onto the remains of the banana.

"They've trained that dog to attack bananas on purpose," said Jack, puzzled. "How did they know we had a banana mascot?"

"I'm scared," said Newton.

"Join the club," said Jack.

"There's a club for scared people?" said Newton.

"No, Newton," said Gretel. "It's just an expression. But if there were one, you'd be the president."

"No, I wouldn't," said Newton. "I'd be too scared. I'm scared of clubs."

Mr. Brainfright backed slowly away from the dog.

Our hearts sank.

But just when it looked like Mr. Brainfright was going to back right off the field, he stopped, ran up, and did a spectacular flip right over the top of Chomp.

As Mr. Brainfright flew over him, Chomp actually cowered. Then he sprang back up, looked around, and began barking. Mr. Brainfright had succeeded — if only for a moment — in confusing his opponent!

The effect on our school was electrifying.

As one, we rose to our feet and rocked the foundations of the Northwest West Stadium with a mighty cheer.

"B-A-N-A-N-A-S!" yelled Mr. Brainfright rising to his feet with us. "LET'S GO BANANAS!"

We all joined in the chant, stomping our feet, the sound echoing under the metal roof like thunder.

For the first time in memory, the Northwest West Academy grandstand was silent.

The sight of a giant banana taunting their mascot may not exactly have struck fear into their hearts, but it had certainly given them something to think about.

At that moment, the PA system crackled into life.

"Welcome to the fiftieth annual Northwest inter-school track-and-field competition!" said Flip Johnson, a sports journalist for the *Northwest Times*, who had called every one of the Northwest competitions since they'd begun fifty years earlier. "Let the games begin!"

We roared as one again.

Northwest West Academy roared right back, only louder.

It was on!

Chapter 37

Go, Newton, Go!

And when I say it was on, I'm not kidding. Northwest Southeast Central School went off like a rocket!

And Newton Hooton was no exception.

The first event was the hundred-yard dash.

"You're up first, Hooton!" growled Mr. Grunt. "Just remember what I taught you."

"What was that?" Newton asked, but Mr. Grunt had already walked off.

We all crowded around him, hoping to provide moral support.

"I can't do this," Newton said as Jenny gently guided him to the starting line. "I can't!"

"Why can't you?" said Jenny.

"I'm scared!"

"But that's good," said Gretel. "If you're scared, you'll run faster."

"That's one of the things I'm scared of," said Newton, crouched and quivering. "What if I run so fast I can't stop?"

"You will," said Jenny. "Remember how we chased the Northwest West Academy bus?"

"Yes." Newton nodded, smiling nervously. "That was fun."

"So is this!" I said. "And don't forget you've visualized this race many times!"

Newton nodded.

"And Mr. Brainfright is on your side!" said Jack. "Just look at him go!"

"Give me a NEWTON!" yelled Mr. Brainfright at the Northwest Southeast Central stand.

"NEWTON!" they roared back.

"Give me HOOTON!"

"HOOTON!" roared the crowd.

"PUT THEM TOGETHER AND WHAT DO YOU GET?"

"NEWTON HOOTON!" roared the crowd. Then, at Mr. Brainfright's instigation, they went into a slow hand-clapping, foot-stomping chant. "NEW ... TON ... HOO ... TON ... NEW ... TON ... HOO ... TON ..."

The syllables of Newton's name echoed around the stadium. The chanting was so loud, it even drowned out Chomp's frenzied barking, despite Mr. Constrictor's best efforts to get him to bark louder.

"Hear that, Newton?" said Jack. "They're chanting your name!"

"I hear it," said Newton, who was crouched on the starting line, a determined look on his face. He was no longer quivering. He looked focused and strong.

"We're now ready for the first event of the day," announced Flip. "The hundred-yard dash."

The starter raised her pistol and fired.

Newton gave a little yelp and took off, crossing the finish line a full two seconds ahead of his nearest Northwest West Academy rival. And he wasn't content with that, either. He kept running.

And running.

And running.

Chapter 38

Stop, Newton, Stop!

"Look at that kid go!" enthused Flip. "He's faster than a *stocking full of rabbits!*"

"I think he might be a bit freaked out by that stupid dog," said Gretel.

"I'll go get him," said Jenny.

"Good idea," said Jack. "We need him. The day has only just started."

And what a start it was!

In the first half hour alone, Newton won both the hundred- and two-hundred-yard dashes, Gretel easily won the shot-put event for her age group, and David took the long jump with ease.

They even managed to stand on the winners' podium without falling off, although Newton was swaying rather violently toward the end of the Northwest Southeast Central anthem, which consisted of Principal Greenbeard playing, "The Good Ship Northwest Southeast Central" on his hornpipe. (It was basically the same tune as "The Good Ship Lollipop" except that we substituted the words, "Northwest Southeast Central School" for the word "lollipop." Yeah, I know — it didn't rhyme any better than Northwest West Academy's anthem did, but it was ours and we loved it.)

Only 5B students, of course, had been on the Brainfright Program for Sporting Excellence, but our early wins — as well as Mr. Brainfright's tireless mascotting — seemed to energize the rest of the school, and similar successes started piling up across all age groups and events.

Even the first grade won its sack race, and if its current form continued, the egg-and-spoon race later in the day was already in the bag.

Poor Chomp was beside himself.

The more we won, the more crazy he became, growling and slobbering and biting at his leash. In fact, at one point he bit right through it and charged straight at Jack.

Jack, who was helping out at the pole-vaulting event, managed to use one of the poles to pole-vault himself to safety by hanging on to the crossbar at the top while Mr. Constrictor reluctantly brought Chomp back under control.

This, of course, only made Chomp even meaner, and madder, than before.

Meanwhile, Flip Johnson was so excited by the day's events that he was having trouble trying to find words to describe what was happening.

"I've *never* seen anything like it!" enthused Flip.

"In the entire *fifty years* of this event, I've never known Northwest Southeast Central to get off to *such* an *amazing* start . . . or to have such an *impressive* mascot! They are certainly giving it everything they've got, and I have a feeling they've only just started! The strongest performers for Northwest Southeast Central so far have been Newton Hooton, who was faster than a *bag full of rattlesnakes* in the hundred-yard dash. In the shot put, Gretel Armstrong proved she was stronger than a *birthday cake with pink icing*, and in the long jump, David Worthy jumped longer than a *rickshaw in a wind tunnel!*"

"A rickshaw in a wind tunnel?" said Jack, who had joined us back in the grandstand. "Can anybody tell me what on *earth* he is talking about?"

I shrugged. "I don't know," I said. "But give the guy a break — he's been doing this for fifty years now!"

"Well, he's making about as much sense as a *grandmother in a phone booth!*" said Jack.

Chapter 39

Flip Johnson's top ten "Flipisms"

1. Faster than a stocking full of rabbits.
2. More off course than a lemming in a shopping mall.
3. Stronger than a birthday cake with pink icing.
4. Louder than a washing machine full of gravel.
5. Higher than a hairdresser on stilts.
6. Hungrier than a barrel full of water buffalo.
7. More determined than a dolphin eating donuts.
8. Slower than a bath plug driving a stolen sports car.
9. More sizzle than a sausage in a solarium.
10. More excited than a lawn mower at a rock concert.

Chapter 40

Troy versus Gretel

Meanwhile, Mr. Brainfright was jumping, clapping, punching, high-kicking, twisting, turning, and somersaulting in an apparently inexhaustible blur of inspired cheerleading.

He was still completely crazy, but in this context his madness made a kind of crazy sense.

Our school loved it. The whole of the Northwest Southeast Central grandstand was imitating his every move — even the teachers.

Then the loudspeakers crackled to life again.

"And now, we come to the final of the javelin toss, where Troy Gurgling and Gretel Armstrong are locked in a titanic battle for first place!" announced Flip. "In the past few years this event has been dominated by Troy Gurgling, but given the form that Gretel Armstrong demonstrated earlier with her shot put, and her amazing showing in the javelin so far, I think there's a good chance we will see that record broken here this morning."

Flip's comments initiated a fresh roar of derision — and a fresh round of plastic- and

118

cardboard-cup-throwing — from the Northwest West Academy stand.

But it was down on the field that the real drama was shaping up.

Troy was standing at the line.

Grant was sitting in the stand with us, holding an enormous plastic ear to the side of his head.

"What's that?" said Jenny.

"It's a Super Ear!" said Grant. "My dad invented it. You can hear what people are saying no matter how far away they are!"

"Wow," said Jenny. "That is SO cool, Grant!"

"What are they saying?" I asked him.

"Well," said Grant, concentrating. "Troy just said, 'Look and learn, Armstrong!' And Gretel said, 'What, learn how *not* to do it?' and Troy said, 'You think you're *so* funny!' And Mr. Constrictor said, 'Come on, Troy, show them what you've got!'"

It was clear from the action on the field that this was one of Grant's invention's that really did work the way it was supposed to.

We could see Troy pawing the ground with his foot like a bull getting ready to charge . . . and then he ran, holding the javelin high above his head.

Flip was beside himself. "Troy Gurgling throws . . . OH, dear! A *terrible* throw! The pressure is obviously too much for Troy this morning. That javelin has gone more off course than a *lemming in a shopping mall*!

119

Let's see if Armstrong can keep her nerve and give it her best."

Gretel walked back to the line, her face a picture of steely resolve.

The Northwest West Academy stand erupted with jeers and boos.

Mr. Brainfright countered this by starting up a javelin-tossing routine and cheer.

"When it comes to throwing metal.
No one can beat Gretel!
She can throw high.
She can throw long.
Give me a cheer
for Gretel Armstrong!"

We cheered so loudly we completely drowned out Northwest West Academy.

Gretel looked up at our stand and smiled.

Then she ran and threw.

We all watched, openmouthed and silent, as the javelin flew longer and higher than any of us had ever seen a javelin fly before.

Flip broke the silence. "It's the most amazing throw I've ever seen. . . . It just keeps going and going. . . . In fact, it's coming toward the commentating booth! Folks, I can see the tip of that javelin, it's shining like a missile, and it's heading straight . . .

for . . . oh, no . . . I don't believe it. . . . It's heading straight . . . for . . . ME!!!"

The javelin smashed through the window of Flip's booth. Through the loudspeaker came a loud sound of shattering glass.

We were horrified.

Nobody made a noise.

Not even the Northwest West Academy students.

Gretel was standing on the field with her hands over her mouth.

"Do you think . . . Flip . . . is . . . ?" said Jack, unable to bring himself to say it.

"Oh, no! Oh, no!" Jenny was saying, wringing her hands.

"What a way to go!" said Jack.

Chapter 41

What a throw!

Suddenly, the PA crackled into life.

"WHAT A THROW!" shouted Flip, as alive as ever. He was leaning out of the front of his booth with the microphone in one hand and the javelin in the other. "LADIES AND GENTLEMEN, Gretel Armstrong has just hurled her javelin — and herself — into Northwest athletic history!"

Mr. Brainfright ran over to Gretel and bent down so she could climb onto his back for a victory lap of the stadium.

Troy and Mr. Constrictor stood dumbfounded on the field, trying to understand what had just happened. Most unusual of all, even Chomp had stopped barking and growling.

Suddenly, Mr. Constrictor came back to life and went over to the judge's table and began waving his arms, shouting and pointing repeatedly at Mr. Brainfright.

"What's he saying, Grant?" I said.

"He wants a re-throw," said Grant, using his Super Ear to track their conversation.

"On what grounds?"

"On the grounds that Troy was distracted by Mr. Brainfright's banana mascotting."

The judges, however, appeared to have other ideas. They were shaking their heads.

Mr. Constrictor began pounding the table and threatening them.

He did this so loudly that we could hear him *without* any help from Grant's Super Ear. He appeared to be appealing the throw on the grounds that if they didn't give Troy a re-throw then he would squeeze them in a variety of unpleasant ways until they popped.

Chapter 42

Top ten Mr. Constrictor threats

1. I'm going to squeeze your head like a pimple until it pops.
2. I'm going to squeeze your head like a blister until it pops.
3. I'm going to squeeze your head like a boil until it pops.
4. I'm going to squeeze your head like a balloon until it pops.
5. I'm going to squeeze your head like a marshmallow until it pops.
6. I'm going to squeeze your head like a bubble wrap bubble in a sheet of bubble wrap until it pops.
7. I'm going to squeeze your head like an empty plastic bag until it pops.
8. I'm going to squeeze your head like a tube of toothpaste until it pops.
9. I'm going to squeeze your head like a grapefruit until it pops.
10. I'm going to squeeze your head like a raw egg until it pops.

Chapter 43

Pimple zapping

But it was to no avail. The judges weren't scared of Mr. Constrictor's threats, so Gretel's throw — and the new Northwest record — stood.

Jenny turned to me and grabbed my arm. "We can do this, Henry," she said, her eyes shining. "For the first time ever, I think we can really win!"

"Of course we can really win," said Mr. Grunt, who had come up behind us. "My cutting-edge training methods are so effective they're even working on you clumsy clots! I really *am* the greatest coach in Northwest! I bet the Northwest All-Stars are sorry now!"

Mr. Grunt strutted off down to the field.

"He really is a . . . very unpleasant man," said Jenny, immediately putting her hand over her mouth, ashamed of having said something nasty.

"It's okay, Jenny," I said, taking her hand away. "That's putting it as nicely as it's possible to put it."

Jenny suddenly grabbed my arm. "Isn't that Fred and Clive?" she said.

"Where?" I said.

"Down there in front of the Northwest West Academy grandstand," she said. "Talking to Mr. Constrictor."

"I think you're right," I said.

"Grant," I said, "point your Super Ear in that direction and tell us what they're saying."

"Pimple cream," said Grant.

"Pimple cream?" said Jenny.

"Yes!" said Grant. "Apparently, Fred is taking a girl out but he's worried about having too many pimples."

"Fred is taking a girl out?" said Jenny incredulously. "What sort of girl would go out with Fred? And why on earth would he be telling Mr. Constrictor about it?"

"Well, apparently Mr. Constrictor knows a great new pimple-zapping cream called Pim-zap, which will zap all of Fred's pimples once and for all."

"Nonsense!" said Jenny. "You're making it up!"

"I'm not making it up!" said Grant. "That's what they're saying!"

"Give me that Super Ear," I said, grabbing it from him and putting it up to my ear.

"That's not them talking," I said. "The Super Ear is picking up interference. You were listening to a radio commercial."

"Well, that would explain it," said Grant. "I guess the Super Ear needs some adjustment. After all, it is only a prototype."

"The thing is," said Jenny, "if Fred and Clive are *not* talking about pimples with Mr. Constrictor, then what *are* they talking about?"

"Beats me," I said. "Maybe they're getting his autograph."

"But he's on the other side," said Jenny.

"He was a pro wrestler, though," I reminded her. "And Fred and Clive and their dad *are* big fans."

"Hmmm . . ." said Jenny unhappily. "They don't *look* like they're autograph-hunting. They don't have pens or paper."

I nodded. She was right. "Maybe they just want to say they've talked to him."

"Talk?" said Jenny. "You mean get shouted at. He looks very upset."

"He always looks upset," I said. "Too much scowling."

"That's quite possible," said Jenny. "My mother says that if you're making a face and the wind changes, you'll be stuck with that face forever."

At that moment Flip Johnson cut in over the top of us. "And now we come to the four-hundred-yard dash, an event traditionally dominated by Northwest West Academy, but with Newton Hooton on a winning streak hotter than a *razor blade in a pot of boiling alligators*, who can tell what's going to happen out there today?"

Chapter 44

Where's Newton?

At that moment Mr. Grunt came running up to us. "Where's Newton Hooton?" he said. "The four-hundred-yard dash is coming up and he's our best runner!"

We looked around, but he was nowhere to be seen.

"He was here a minute ago," I said.

"I hope he's all right," said Jenny.

"Maybe the pressure got to be too much for him," I said.

"Too much pressure?" said Mr. Grunt. "I'll give him too much pressure if he doesn't present himself at the starting line in five minutes' time!"

"I'll check underneath all the benches," said Gretel.

"I'll check outside the stadium," said Jenny, "in case he's decided to make a run for it."

"I'll check inside Chomp's stomach," said Jack. "Just in case."

"That's not funny," I said.

Jack and I searched everywhere. Well, everywhere except inside Chomp's stomach. We were on the far side of the stadium, where nobody was sitting, when we walked past a trash can.

"Henry," Jack said, "can I ask you a question?"

"What is it?" I said.

"Do trash cans have eyes?"

"Not usually," I said.

"Then I think we've found Newton." Jack pointed to a trash can with two eyeballs visible through the holes near the top.

"Newton?" I said. "What are you doing in there?"

"Hiding," he replied.

"Well, we've found you now," said Jack, "so you'd better come out. Your next race is about to start."

"That's why I'm hiding," said Newton. "I can't run in that race."

"Why not?" I said.

"Because I'm scared."

"Scared of losing?" I said.

"No," said Newton. "Scared of winning!"

"But you don't have to be scared of winning," said Jack. "You've already stood on top of the winners' podium a few times today and you didn't fall off."

"I'm not scared of that anymore," said Newton.

"Then what?" I said.

"Fred and Clive Durkin," said Newton. "I was

129

going to the locker rooms and they grabbed me and told me they would squeeze my head until it popped if I won the race."

"But why would they do that?" said Jack. "They're on our side!"

"Maybe," I said. "And then again, maybe not."

Suddenly, I realized the truth.

There was no time to lose.

"Jack," I said, "I need you and Gretel and Jenny to form a guard around Newton and protect him when he finishes the race. Don't let anybody hurt him. Okay?"

"Got it," said Jack, frowning, "but . . . Henry . . . you're not going to do anything stupid, are you?"

"I'll try not to," I said, running off to find Fred and Clive.

But I was.

I was going to do the stupidest and most dangerous thing possible.

I was going to have a little talk with Fred and Clive Durkin.

Alone.

Chapter 45

Henry versus Fred, round 1

It didn't take me long to find them.

They had Penny and Gina up against a wall, and although I couldn't hear what they were saying, I could see that Penny and Gina were clearly frightened.

I came up behind Fred and Clive. "Let them go!" I said. "And their horses, too."

Fred and Clive turned around and stared at me in surprise.

Penny and Gina sensibly took the opportunity to jump on their imaginary horses and gallop off.

"Well, well, well," said Fred, an evil smile on his face. "If it isn't my old friend Henry McThrottle."

"I'm not your *old friend*, Fred," I said.

"I think you need to learn some manners, Henry. Don't you think so, Clive?"

"Definitely," said Clive. "He can be very rude."

"I don't need a manners lesson," I said. "And if I did, you'd be the last person I'd come to!"

The smile disappeared from Fred's face. "Have you got a problem, McThrottle?" he said.

"Yes," I said. "I've got a big problem."

"You can say that again," said Clive.

"Shut up, Clive," said Fred. "Henry's trying to tell us his problem."

"What did you say to Newton Hooton?" I asked.

Fred looked blank. "Nothing."

"Then why was he hiding in a trash can?" I said.

"I don't know!" said Fred, unable to resist a smirk. "Maybe because that's where he belongs."

"Good one, Fred!" said Clive.

"Or maybe you told him that if he won his next race you'd squeeze his head until it popped, just like your hero, The Boa."

"What are you getting at?" said Fred.

"I know you're working for Mr. Constrictor. I saw you talking to him."

"We were just getting his autograph, weren't we, Clive?"

Clive nodded.

"You didn't have pens or paper," I said. "And how come you've never been hit by any of the bus attacks in the school yard? Because you knew they were coming! And how did Mr. Constrictor know to train Chomp to attack bananas? You told him about Mr. Brainfright, that's how! And now that we're winning for the first time ever, Mr. Constrictor has told you to go around threatening everybody on our team. Well, you're not getting away with it. Because I'm going to tell Principal

132

Greenbeard. You're going down, Durkin — you and your stupid brother!"

"Hey!" said Clive. "I'm not stupid!"

"Yes, you are," Fred said to Clive. Then he turned to me. "Are you quite finished, McThrottle?"

My heart was thumping.

I was panting.

I was sweating.

I was feeling a strange feeling in my stomach.

But I wasn't finished.

Not quite.

"Wait until everybody finds out," I said. "You won't be Fred 'Goody Two-shoes' Durkin anymore. Finally, everybody will know what you're really like."

Fred smiled. "Have you finished *now*, McThrottle?"

"Yes," I said.

"Any last words before Fred and I squeeze your head until it pops?" said Clive, advancing toward me, his hands outstretched.

"No, no, no, little brother," said Fred, putting his arm out to stop Clive. "No squeezing."

"No squeezing?" said Clive. "Are you feeling all right?"

"I'm fine," said Fred. "Never felt better. Henry, if you think you must tell Principal Greenbeard what you think you know, then that's what you must do. Despite what you might think of me, I respect your

133

honesty. In fact, I'm inspired. If you tell Principal Greenbeard everything you know, then I'm going to tell him — and the Northwest Police — everything I know about you."

"You don't have anything on me!" I said.

"Are you so sure, Henry?" he said. "After all, I do know something about that banana suit."

"Banana suit?" I said. "I don't know what you're talking about. You're just bluffing."

"Am I?" said Fred.

"Are you?" said Clive.

"If you've got something to tell me, then spit it out," I said.

"Remember that tanker that ran off the road and crashed into the Banana Emporium?" said Fred.

My heart started pounding again. My sweat started sweating. "I don't know what you're talking about!" I said, but this time I was lying. I knew exactly what he was talking about. The question was, how much did he know?

"Ah, but I think you do," said Fred. "Care to tell me the real reason that tanker ran off the road?"

"It was an accident," I said.

"It was no accident," said Fred. "I saw the whole thing!"

"Me too," said Clive.

"You weren't even there," said Fred.

"Oh," said Clive.

"You're lying, Fred," I said.

But for once Fred was definitely not lying. He knew everything. The whole sorry story.

"You won't tell anybody, will you?" I said.

"Of course not," said Fred. "Wouldn't dream of it . . . unless you do something silly, of course. . . . Do we have an understanding?"

"Yes," I said. "We have an understanding."

"Understanding is good," said Fred. "It's good when friends understand each other. Now get out of my sight, McThrottle."

Chapter 46

Newton's bodyguards

As I walked back to our grandstand I wasn't sure what I'd achieved — if anything — by going to visit Fred and Clive.

I had wanted to find out if they were working for Mr. Constrictor, and if so, to make them stop.

So now I knew for sure that they were working for Mr. Constrictor, and they knew that I knew, but I couldn't stop them because Fred knew too much about me. And even worse, he now *knew* that I knew that he knew too much.

Confused? It wasn't that difficult, really.

What it boiled down to was that if I spilled the beans on Fred, he would spill the beans on me, and I couldn't possibly risk that.

So I was under Fred's thumb.

And one thing I didn't like being was under anybody's thumb, especially Fred's.

As I took my seat back in the grandstand, I was still in such a state of shock that I barely even noticed that down on the field Newton was coming up the home stretch for his four-hundred-yard dash.

The crowd was roaring.

And so was Flip Johnson. "And Newton Hooton is dominating this race!" he said with excitement. "He's running faster than a *dandelion in a pink dress*! Go, Newton, go!"

"NO, NEWTON, NO!" I yelled.

I was worried about Newton, but to tell you the truth, I was even more worried about myself. If Newton won this race, Fred and Clive would hold *me* responsible.

But it was too late. Newton went streaming across the finish line, a full three seconds ahead of the nearest Northwest West Academy runner.

As he did, Jack, Gretel, and Jenny closed in around him in a tight circle and escorted him safely to the winners' podium in preparation for yet another climb to the top.

The crowd went wild.

Flip Johnson went wild.

Mr. Brainfright went wild.

And Mr. Constrictor went wild, too. But Mr. Constrictor didn't go *good*-wild. He went *wild*-wild.

He'd clearly been counting on Fred and Clive's threats to stop our winning streak dead in its tracks. But, like his bus attacks, his banana-hating dog, and his attempts to intimidate the judges, it hadn't worked.

As Mr. Brainfright started up a victory chant in

front of our grandstand, Mr. Constrictor came surging across the field toward him.

He was flanked by Troy Gurgling on one side and the slobbering, teeth-gnashing Chomp on the other.

I wasn't sure what he was up to exactly, but I did know one thing — he hadn't come to shake Mr. Brainfright's hand.

Chapter 47

Constrictor versus Brainfright

"Hey, Brainfright!" snarled Mr. Constrictor. "Turn around and fight like a man!"

Mr. Brainfright stopped dancing and turned around. "Fight you? Whatever for? And fight you like a man? Why, that's impossible! I'm a banana!"

"Are you trying to be funny?" said Mr. Constrictor, moving his face menacingly close to Mr. Brainfright's banana head.

"No," said Mr. Brainfright. "My job is to inspire my school."

"Is it really?" said Mr. Constrictor. "I could have sworn your intention was to distract and confuse my school with your stupid antics."

"I'm sorry you feel that way," said Mr. Brainfright. "But every team has a right to have a mascot. And your dog is no angel. You may not realize this, but he's actually very frightening to some of our students."

"What do you mean?" said Mr. Constrictor, whose upper lip was curling in a very frightening way . . . much like Chomp's.

"Well, the way he snarls and slobbers," said Mr. Brainfright, "he looks quite . . . dangerous . . . like those teeth of his would really hurt. . . ."

"Are you saying my dog's aggressive?" said Mr. Constrictor as Chomp made yet another lunge for Mr. Brainfright's legs.

"Not at all!" said Mr. Brainfright, stepping backward. "I'm just saying —"

"If you insult my dog, you insult me!" said Mr. Constrictor.

"If you'll just let me finish —" said Mr. Brainfright. "It's just that —"

But Mr. Constrictor was in no mood to let Mr. Brainfright finish. He handed Chomp's leash to Troy, and opened his arms wide.

At first I thought he was embracing Mr. Brainfright, but when I heard the high-pitched gurgling noise coming from Mr. Brainfright's throat I realized the truth.

Mr. Brainfright was being squeezed!

"I'll give your *brain* a *fright* all right, Mr. Brainfright!" roared Mr. Constrictor. "I'm going to squeeze your brain until it pops!"

"And it looks like the action is heating up on the field," announced Flip, who didn't seem to question or care what he commentated on, as long as he was commentating. "It's Karl — *The Boa* — Constrictor versus Mr. Brainfright, the giant banana. I wouldn't like to

140

try to second-guess the outcome here, because any- thing could happen, but The Boa has the banana in a squeeze and I'm not sure what the banana's got to match that."

A large crowd had gathered.

Mr. Brainfright was doing his best to escape, but he was helpless in his banana suit.

Fred and Clive were at the front, thrilled at having a ringside seat to see their hero in full squeezing mode.

David was pointing to his handbook. "This is *definitely* against the rules!"

But the only response was from Chomp, who lunged at David, took the book out of his hands, and swallowed it whole.

"Somebody stop him!" said Jenny.

"It's too late!" said David. "He's already swallowed it!"

"Not Chomp, you idiot!" said Jenny. "Mr. Constrictor! He's killing Mr. Brainfright!"

Chapter 48

Squeezed!

Jenny was right.

Mr. Brainfright was making a sound unlike any banana I'd ever heard. Or any human for that matter. And I'd never heard Jenny call anybody an idiot before.

This was definitely serious.

Not only were we watching the best teacher we'd ever had being squeezed to death, but we were watching our chances of winning being squeezed away, second by excruciating second!

"Clear a path!" said a powerful voice. "Let me through."

It was Gretel!

Which was good.

If anyone could save Mr. Brainfright from The Boa, it was her.

She wrapped her powerful arms around Mr. Constrictor and, with great effort, dragged him off Mr. Brainfright's limp, banana-suited body.

Fred and Clive looked disappointed beyond words. "You are such a spoilsport, Armstrong," said Fred.

"Yeah," said Clive. "It's not fair! You've got to let The Boa do his thing!"

Gretel ignored them.

She released her grip on Mr. Constrictor and he turned to face her.

"You've got some nerve," he said in a menacing voice. "You've got some *real* nerve . . . plus a very strong grip. I admire that. . . . even if you do play for the wrong team. I don't suppose you'd consider changing schools? You'd be very welcome at Northwest West Academy."

Gretel didn't answer — she just glared at him.

"I'll take that as a no," he said. "But let me know if you ever change your mind."

Then he turned away from her. "Troy!" he boomed. "Bring Chomp and let's get out of here."

Troy, who seemed just as scared of the growling, leash-biting Chomp as we all were, walked over to Mr. Constrictor and they both headed back toward the Northwest West Academy grandstand.

They were greeted by a rousing cheer.

At that same moment, Mr. Brainfright let out a moan of pain.

"Are you all right, Mr. Brainfright?" said Jenny, who was kneeling beside him on the ground.

"No," said Mr. Brainfright. "I don't think so. It feels like I've been squeezed!"

"You have been!" said Gretel. "By Mr. Constrictor."

"Well, that would explain it then," said Mr. Brainfright.

"Can you get up?" said Jack.

"I don't think so," said Mr. Brainfright. "My whole body feels numb."

We looked at each other.

This was bad.

Like an angel sent from heaven, Mrs. Bandaid appeared among us.

"Excuse me," she called out, pushing her way through the crowd. "Mobile Band-Aid unit coming through! Stand clear!"

She was carrying a large metal box, like a carpenter or builder would use for their tools. But hers was white with a large red cross on the lid, and when she opened it, its tiered shelves revealed an amazing display of Band-Aids. There were Band-Aids of all shapes and sizes — round ones, square ones, little ones, patterned ones, and even waterproof ones.

"Oh, my goodness," she said, looking at Mr. Brainfright. "Oh, dear."

"What is it?" said Mr. Brainfright. "Is it serious?"

"Very serious," said Mrs. Bandaid. "You need a Band-Aid. In fact, you need *lots* of Band-Aids! But first you'll have to get out of that suit."

"But I can't!" said Mr. Brainfright. "I'm the Northwest Southeast Central mascot! The competition's not over yet. We still have the decathlon! They need me!"

"Well," said Mrs. Bandaid, removing Mr. Brainfright's head, "you're not going to be much use to them in your present condition. You'll have to find somebody else to do it."

"But there *is* nobody else," I said. "Only Mr. Brainfright can do it!"

"Listen to me, Henry," said Mrs. Bandaid. "Mr. Brainfright is very badly squashed. If I don't get some Band-Aids on him soon, he may not pull through at all. Now help me get this suit off! Please!"

I nodded, knelt down, and helped Mr. Brainfright out of his suit. He'd been dancing for a long time, and I'm not sure how long he'd had the suit on before today, but he sure smelled bad. Not unlike a rotten banana.

"Thanks, Henry," said Mr. Brainfright. "I'm really sorry about this. Can you take over the mascotting for me?"

"Me?" I said. "You want *me* to be the banana mascot?"

"Yes," said Mr. Brainfright, "why not?"

"Because I don't know the first thing about it!" I said. "That's why not. You're a hard act to follow, Mr. Brainfright. I couldn't inspire anybody — I'd only make them laugh."

"It's really not *that* difficult," said Mr. Brainfright.

"I'm sorry," I said, "but I just can't."

At that moment Flip's voice came over the loudspeaker. "Goodness me, ladies and gentlemen, what a turnaround for Northwest West Academy! They are blitzing this competition just like the Northwest West Academy of old, while the Northwest Southeast Central mascot lies injured on the field. Northwest West Academy has already racked up convincing wins in the hurdles and the high jump, while the first graders have easily won the hotly contested egg-and-spoon race! This contest is not over yet, though — the scores are almost even and it looks like the decathlon will be the deciding event of the day."

"I'm scared," said Newton. "I'm *really* scared."

"We all are, Newton," said Jenny, patting his arm. "We all are."

Chapter 49

If the suit fits . . .

"Let's see who else the suit fits," said Gretel. She tried to put one of her powerful arms into the sleeve, but it was too tight. "It's too small for me."

She passed it to Newton.

"I'm too scared to wear it," he said, passing it to Jack.

"It's too wide," he said, wrapping it around his skinny body. He gave the suit to Jenny.

"*Much* too big for me," she said.

Gretel took the suit back and held it up in front of me. "Henry!" she said. "It's your size exactly!"

"Nah," I said. "The head is all wrong."

"No, it's not," said Gretel. "Your head is actually a bit banana-shaped, you know."

"Look," I said, ignoring Gretel's insult, "even if it *did* fit, I'm not putting it on. What about mascot madness?"

"You won't be in it for long enough," said Gretel. "There's only the decathlon left. You need to wear a suit for hours for mascot madness to take hold."

"I can't!" I said.

"But we'll lose if you don't!" said Jenny.

"But I have to write my report!"

"What report?" said Jenny. "That Northwest Southeast Central was beaten by Northwest West Academy again? You don't have to waste any time writing that report — just use last year's and change the date."

"You don't understand," I said. "I don't mean I won't. . . . I mean I *CAN'T*!"

"My mother says there's no such word as *can't*," said Jenny.

"She's right," said Mr. Brainfright.

"She's wrong," I said. "I think it's time to tell you the truth about why I can't possibly be the banana mascot."

"Yes," said Jenny. "I think you'd better."

I took a deep breath and began my story.

Chapter 50

The truth

"One summer I got a job as a promotional mascot for the Northwest Banana Emporium," I began. "It was my job to stand outside and wave at the passing traffic."

"Wow, what a dream job." Jenny sighed. "I love waving. Why did you ever leave?"

I took a deep breath. "Well," I said, "everything was good and banana sales were increasing . . . until one unfortunate day when a tanker driver was so startled by the sight of a giant banana waving at him that he lost control of his vehicle and crashed into the Banana Emporium."

"Was anybody hurt?" said Jenny.

"Incredibly, no," I said, "but, given the amount of banana skins in the Emporium, it took at least ten minutes for the truck to stop skidding. By that time, it had left a trail of destruction from one end of Northwest to the other."

"I remember that!" said Jack. "But I didn't know it was your fault!"

"Nobody did. The driver had a concussion and couldn't remember what caused the accident. After it happened, I just ran. I threw the suit over a fence into a vacant lot and just kept on running."

"So that's how Mr. Brainfright came to find it!" said Newton.

I nodded. "Yes — and that's why I can't be the mascot. I'm afraid to put that suit back on."

"Henry," said Jenny, "that was a terrible thing to happen, for sure, but it's in the past."

"Easy for you to say."

"Maybe," she said, "but I do know one thing: Until you put that suit back on you're never truly going to conquer your fear. Is that how you want to go through life? Afraid to put on a banana suit?"

"I've done okay so far," I pointed out.

"But not today," said Jenny. "Because if you don't put that suit on now, something much more terrible is going to happen."

"What could be more terrible than causing a tanker to run off the road and half of Northwest to be destroyed?"

"For that bunch of bad sports at Northwest West Academy to win after we've come so close to beating them!" she said. "We still have a chance, Henry, but only if you put on the suit. Besides, you're the only one who's had experience as a banana!"

"I don't know. . . ." I said.

Jenny held the suit out toward me. "Well? Will you do it, Henry?"

I wanted to.

I really did.

But I was scared.

Mr. Brainfright looked up at me pleadingly. "Please, Henry," he said. "I'm not sure how much time I have left . . . but if I could live long enough to see a Northwest Southeast Central School victory, it will all have been worthwhile!"

Chapter 51

The true truth

Jenny held the suit open for me.

I was scared, but how could I refuse the request of a man who had been squeezed by *The Boa*?

After all Mr. Brainfright had done for us, it didn't seem like so much to ask.

Well, it *was* a lot to ask, but I couldn't say no.

"Okay," I said.

"Thank you, Henry!" said Mr. Brainfright, smiling as he closed his eyes.

I put one foot down into the suit and out through the stockinged leg, and then the other.

"Well done," said Jenny.

"Looking good," said Gretel as I pushed my arms into the sleeves.

"Thanks," I said. "Can you zip me up?"

"I'll do it," said Jack.

I took a deep breath.

There was no turning back now.

Jack zipped the suit up.

"And now for the head," said Newton. "Are you ready?"

"I think so," I said, kneeling.

Newton solemnly placed the banana head down over my own. As it came to rest on my shoulders, I heard a cheer go up from our stand.

"And as the final competitors prepare for the last event of the day — the decathlon," said Flip, "the injured Mr. Brainfright has passed the baton to the brave Henry McThrottle. Let's hope for their team's sake that McThrottle can continue the high standard of banana mascotting that we have seen here today and that he's got what it takes to push Northwest Southeast Central over the line so they can claim their first-ever victory in this competition."

"So, Henry, how does it feel?" asked Jenny.

I stood there for a moment. The suit felt heavy. And hot.

"I don't know," I finally said. "It feels weird. I don't think I can do this."

"Sure you can," said Jack. "Walk around a bit. You just need to get used to it again."

I took a few tentative steps.

"Now punch the air!" said Gretel.

I punched the air.

"That's great, Henry!" said Jenny. "Now try the other arm!"

I shrugged and punched the air with my other arm.

"Now try a somersault," said Newton.

I bent over, lost my balance, and fell in a heap on the ground.

The Northwest West grandstand erupted with laughter, jeers, and a fresh round of trash throwing.

I tried to get up, but the suit was too heavy and I fell back down.

I looked up at the disappointed faces of my classmates. "I'm sorry," I said, pulling off the head. "I just can't get the accident out of my mind."

"What accident?" said Fiona, who had just arrived back from the locker rooms, and hadn't heard my confession.

"Oh, nothing," I said. "Nothing at all, really. Just a teensy-weensy little mistake I made when I dressed up as a banana and caused a tanker to run off the road, smash into the Banana Emporium, and then destroy half of Northwest. No big deal. Just another great day in the life of Henry Mc CLUMSY-CLOT Throttle."

"The tanker accident? At the Banana Emporium?" said Fiona. "You didn't cause that."

"Of course I did!" I said. "I was there! I should know!"

"And I know for a fact that you had nothing to do with it!" said Fiona. "My father is an accident investigator. He prepared the official report and concluded

154

beyond any doubt that it was caused by a faulty brake line on the tanker."

"He shows you his official reports?" said Jack.

"Of course," said Fiona. "I check his calculations."

"And you're sure there was nothing in that report about a boy in a banana suit?" I said.

"No," said Fiona. "Nothing at all."

I couldn't believe it!

I was innocent!

Freed from the heavy burden of guilt that I'd been carrying for so long, I felt light and happy. Before I knew it I was somersaulting all around the field.

Even the Northwest West Academy students seemed to enjoy that. I could tell they were enjoying themselves because, although they continued to yell insulting comments, they stopped throwing things while I somersaulted.

I jumped, kicked, punched, somersaulted, chanted, borrowed some of Mr. Brainfright's routines and invented a few new ones of my own. I even fell over a few times, but now it didn't seem to matter what I did.

Northwest Southeast Central School was lapping it up, enjoying every minute of my crazy, completely unrehearsed attempt at banana mascotting. I turned around to look at my classmates.

They were standing where I'd left them, but now Mr. Brainfright was standing with them, supported by Jack and Gretel.

His eyes were shining with pride. "Great work, Henry!" he called. "You're a complete natural!"

Chapter 52

Chomp

About the only person who didn't seem to be enjoying my mascotting was Mr. Constrictor. And there was Chomp, of course, who had been trained to *hate* bananas.

Maybe that's why he succeeded in breaking free of his leash again.

Or more likely, why Mr. Constrictor, utterly desperate now in the face of all his failed attempts to stop us, deliberately unleashed him.

I guess I'll never know the truth about how Chomp escaped.

What I do know for sure, though, is what he looked like as he raced across the field toward me.

Chapter 53

What Chomp looked like as he raced across the field toward me

UTTERLY TERRIFYING!

Chapter 54

Chomp versus Henry

I did the only thing possible in the circumstances.

I ran.

As fast as I could.

Or more accurately, I *attempted* to run as fast as I could.

It wasn't easy running in a banana suit, but the sight of Chomp's narrowed eyes, glistening muscles, large pointy teeth, and twin streams of drool flying backward in the wind was all the motivation I needed.

Well, that and the memory of the lesson that Mr. Brainfright had given us about what to do when you're being chased by wild animals.

Chapter 55

Mr. Brainfright's important lesson no. 3

When you're being chased by wild animals, RUN!

Chapter 56

Death-cathlon part 1

At that moment the decathlon, which would be the deciding event of the day, was about to start.

The competitors were all crouched at the starting line ready for the first event, the hundred-yard dash.

The race official had his starting pistol in the air.

"On your marks!" he said. "Ready . . . set . . ."

But before he could say "go," the crowd roared. The competitors, distracted, looked behind them and saw me — and Chomp — speeding around the track toward them.

The looks of terror on their faces said it all.

They abandoned their starting positions and scattered in all directions.

The official, apparently as scared as everybody else, accidentally fired his pistol.

The decathlon had officially started!

The crowd roared again as I raced down the track, Chomp hot on my heels.

There was no time to wave or clown around, though. I was running for my life. I didn't have to imagine there was a wild beast after me, either, as in Mr. Brainfright's visualization sessions — there really *was* a wild beast after me!

As I crossed the finish line, the crowd roared once more.

"Ladies and gentlemen!" shouted Flip. "We have just witnessed the fastest-ever hundred-yard dash in the history of this competition! Unbelievable running from Henry McThrottle, in this, the first event of the decathlon. Closely followed by Chomp, from Northwest West Academy. And they're not going to stop there! They're heading toward the long-jump pit, the second event in the decathlon! Looks like they're going for a doubleheader! Two events for the price of one!"

Flip was right. We were headed toward the long-jump pit. But I wasn't the slightest bit interested in breaking running records or going for a doubleheader.

I just wanted to get away from Chomp!

I raced toward the long-jump pit.

Chomp was panting hard. I turned around, but I couldn't see him. Then I looked down. He was right on my tail!

There was no time to think.

I jumped.

The crowd roared.

"What a magnificent jump!" yelled Flip. "Longer than a *spaghettified pipe cleaner*!"

But it wasn't long enough to get away from Chomp.

The crowd roared again.

"Another magnificent jump!" shouted Flip. "I've never seen a dog jump like that! Or a banana, for that matter!"

"That's my boy, Chomp!" yelled Mr. Constrictor from the other side of the field. "Kill!"

I was pretty sure ordering your mascot to kill the opposing team's mascot was against the rule book, but as Chomp had swallowed it, and as I was running for my life, it wasn't exactly possible to check.

I looked around me.

I was heading toward the shot-put circle.

There was a pile of the heavy metal balls in the middle.

I sprinted for them, trying to put as much distance between me and Chomp as possible. I reached the balls, leaped over them, and turned to face Chomp.

I picked one up and lobbed it at him. It shot out of my hand with the speed and power of a cannonball.

Chomp darted left.

I picked up and launched another one.

Chomp darted right, straightened, and then sprang through the air straight at me.

There was no time left.

I had to do this, and do it right.

I picked up the third and final ball, focused and hurled it with all my strength right at Chomp's open slobbering mouth.

Chomp just swallowed it whole, as if it were no more than a tasty snack.

"Look at that!" enthused Flip. "Not only are we seeing the world's fastest decathlon out here today, but we're seeing some world-class shot putting and shot swallowing! That dog is hungrier than a *barrel full of water buffalo!*"

I kept running.

So did Chomp, although he was slightly slower than before, thanks to the added weight of the shot in his stomach.

I ran toward the high jump.

Chomp ran after me.

I jumped.

Chomp jumped — not as high as me, but high enough to clear the bar.

The crowd roared. Both schools were going wild in support of their mascots.

"It's *mascot madness* out there today!" shouted Flip. "Absolute *mascot madness!*"

I hit the track and ran around the outside, waving my arms, pleading for somebody to help me.

But everybody just waved their arms back, thinking I was mascotting.

If only they could have seen my face, they would have seen the truth.

But all they could see was the big smiling face of the banana.

Chapter 57

Death-cathlon part 2

The rest of the chase is pretty much a blur.

Somehow, as I ran for my life and Chomp ran for mine, we not only managed to complete each one of the decathlon's ten events in the correct order, but we also broke each of the pre-existing records for each event.

We smashed the 400-yard-dash record.

We blew the hurdling record out of the water.

I threw a discus at Chomp and ended up throwing it farther than a discus had ever been thrown in the Northwest stadium. Chomp matched my achievement, however, by swallowing the first discus in Northwest sports history.

I broke both speed and distance records for javelin throwing after hurling a javelin aimed at Chomp's heart. Chomp kept pace, however, by breaking both javelin-catching and javelin-chomping records, reducing the javelin to splinters only moments after launching himself into the air for a spectacular midair javelin catch.

After reducing all the previous 1500-yard-dash records to rubble, I knew I couldn't run much longer.

I was getting tired.

The banana suit was heavy.

And Chomp, despite having swallowed a shot and a discus, was gaining on me.

Any moment now, he was going to catch me, leap on top of me, and rip me — and the suit — to shreds.

The more tired I became, however, the more energized the crowd seemed to grow.

I stumbled and the Northwest West Academy grandstand erupted.

"KILL! KILL! KILL!" they chanted, just in case Chomp needed any reminding about the reason he was chasing me.

"And they're on the home stretch, now," said Flip. "There's only one event left to complete in this decathlon — the pole vault!"

My heart leaped.

This was my chance to get away from Chomp once and for all.

If Jack could pole himself to safety, then so could I!

Chomp was getting closer.

And closer.

And closer.

Despite my exhaustion, I grabbed a pole, ran down the track, planted the pole firmly on the ground, and launched myself up into the air.

It was a perfect pole vault . . . well, at least to begin with.

Unfortunately, Chomp lunged at me at the exact moment I left the ground and he managed to sink his teeth deep into the bottom of my banana suit.

Up, up, up we went.

A perfect boy-and-dog pole vault — the first ever in pole-vaulting history!

We cleared the bar and fell onto the mat on the other side.

Chomp and I both sat there for a few moments, dazed and confused, before we regained our senses.

"KILL!" came the command from the Northwest West Academy grandstand — a command that Chomp was only too eager to obey.

Chapter 58

Mascot massacre

I don't know if you've ever had a vicious, shot-swallowing, discus-eating, javelin-chomping attack dog leap at your throat, but let me tell you it's an ugly sight.

I'm happy to say that I can't tell you what it *feels* like, though, because with my last reserves of energy I pulled my banana head off, unzipped the suit, and dived out.

Just in time.

Chomp pounced on top of the suit and began tearing it to pieces.

It was ugly.

Forget mascot madness — this was *mascot massacre*.

Chapter 59

Mr. Grunt has a big fall

And that's how I, Henry McThrottle, the most average athlete at Northwest Southeast Central School, came to break more records in a single day than any other athlete in the Northwest region ever.

That's if you don't count Chomp, and I don't think you should because he is a dog.

A nasty dog with a bad temper who hates bananas.

And just in case anybody doubted just how much he hated bananas, Chomp proved it that afternoon by ripping that suit into a million tiny pieces.

By the time Chomp was finished, it was nothing but a sad pile of banana-colored confetti.

But enough about me and Chomp and the banana suit. What you really want to know is whether Northwest Southeast Central School won, don't you?

Well, nobody knew for a long time.

As well as a great amount of yellow confetti blowing around the stadium, there was a great deal of confusion, table-thumping, and shouting.

The main problem was that while I had achieved record-breaking times and distances in the ten decathlon events, so had Chomp.

Mr. Grunt tried arguing that because Chomp was a dog that none of his points counted, but his objections were overruled by the judges, who argued that there was nothing in the rules to say that dogs couldn't compete in the events.

Mr. Constrictor argued that Chomp should be awarded *double* points for his achievements because of the increased difficulty due to his being a dog, but the judges overruled that argument as well. They decided that a record was a record, whether broken by a dog or a human, and that it would be awarded the same points no matter who — or what — broke it.

Eventually a tense silence fell upon the stadium as the judges deliberated and tallied up the final points for the day.

The silence was broken only by Chomp's frenzied chewing as he chased the flurries of yellow confetti around the ground.

Then Flip Johnson recommenced his commentating. "Well," he said with a sigh, "as we await the judges' final decision, the atmosphere here is as tense as a *cat on ice skates*. Has the new, improved Northwest Southeast Central School been able to gain all the points it needs to win the event for the first time ever? Or has Northwest West Academy's late comeback —

thanks to the extraordinary efforts of Chomp in that amazing decathlon — enabled them to hang on to the cup that has been in their trophy cabinet for forty-nine years?"

"Doesn't he ever stop talking?" asked Jack.

"That's his job," said Gretel.

"And that was my job," said Mr. Brainfright, who was sadly watching a handful of yellow banana suit confetti trail from his fingers. "I loved that suit. I loved being a banana."

We all looked at one another.

It was hard to know what to say.

I mean, we understood how he felt, but we liked him much better as Mr. Brainfright.

At that moment, a blast of feedback squealed through the stadium.

A judge was standing at the presentation table, tapping the microphone, and looking rather alarmed at the noise she had just created.

She leaned into the microphone. "IS THIS THING ON?" she said, and her voice came out even louder than the feedback.

We all put our fingers in our ears as Principal Greenbeard dived to adjust the volume on the PA.

"Sorry about that," said the judge. "Ahh . . . um . . . I would like to congratulate all the participants here today on a truly inspiring competition. In an ideal world we would be able to award a cup to each of the

172

schools, but alas, it is our tough job to award it to only one. And after much deliberation, we have come to a decision. After careful checking of the point tallies for each school, we are very pleased to announce that Northwest Southeast Central School has won by one point — thanks to the heroic efforts of Henry McThrottle, who was awarded extra points for his extraordinary pole vault because of the weight handicap represented by the Northwest West Academy mascot!"

The Northwest Southeast Central School grandstand erupted with the sound of cheering and foot-stomping.

"NOOOOOOOOOOO!!!" screamed Mr. Constrictor. He dropped to his knees and beat the ground with his fists.

Chomp started howling.

Troy Gurgling started crying.

Fiona and David were making their way to the judge's stand to accept the cup on our school's behalf when they were roughly pushed aside by Mr. Grunt.

"Out of my way!" he shouted as he grabbed the cup out of the judge's hands and climbed up onto the podium.

"I'd just like to say a big thanks to MYSELF," he boomed in a voice that had no need of a microphone. "If it wasn't for my cutting-edge training methods none of this would have been possible. I mean, to be

173

able to have beaten a team as good as Northwest West Academy with a bunch of no-hopers like Northwest Southeast Central School, well, it defies belief and proves beyond a doubt what a truly great coach I really am!"

"Doesn't he ever stop boasting?" Jack asked incredulously.

"No," said Gretel. "That's his job. That's what he does."

"Well, I wish he'd stop," said Jack, "because he's making me very angry!"

As it turned out, Jack got his wish almost immediately.

Whether it was the excitement or the weight of the cup, I can't be sure — all I know is that at that moment his "finely honed sense of balance" suddenly deserted him, and he fell face-first off the podium.

The cup flew out of his hands and landed on the grass in front of him.

"Serves him right," said Jack.

Chapter 60

A dream come true

David and Fiona picked up the cup from where it had fallen, cleaned off the confetti and grass, and together held it up high above their heads.

We cheered again.

Needless to say, none of us offered to help Mr. Grunt up.

Well, none of *us*, anyway.

Help for Mr. Grunt came from a very unexpected quarter.

"Here," said Mr. Constrictor, reaching out his hand and pulling Mr. Grunt to his feet.

Mr. Grunt looked embarrassed . . . and slightly scared. "Oh, er . . . Mr. Constrictor," he said. "I'm sorry you lost. But, congratulations on coming in second."

Mr. Constrictor snorted. "Second place is just another word for first loser. You and I both know that, Grunt."

Mr. Grunt looked uncomfortable. "Well . . . er . . . that's certainly one way of looking at it. . . ." he mumbled.

"I've had my eye on you, Grunt," said Mr. Constrictor, "and I like what I see. I'd be interested to hear more about these cutting-edge techniques of yours."

Mr. Grunt tried to look modest, but failed. His chest puffed out and he said, "Oh, well, you see . . . when you've been around for as long as I have, you pick up a few tricks. . . . I was in the Olympics, you know."

"I'm well aware of that," said Mr. Constrictor. "Did you really mean what you said up there about us being a good team?"

"Are you kidding?" gushed Mr. Grunt. "You're the best! You've been the best for forty-nine years! Everybody knows that. Of course, my methods *are* powerful, but even so, it's taken a long time for them to take effect, given the hopelessness of what I've had to work with."

Mr. Constrictor nodded his agreement. "How would you like to come and work with a real team?" he said. "I could use a man like you, Grunt. With the raw talent of the Northwest West Academy students and your cutting-edge training methods, there's no reason why we shouldn't dominate this competition for the next forty-nine years! I want to see you on our team tomorrow and that cup returned to our cabinet next year. What do you say? Do you need time to think about it?"

"None at all," said Mr. Grunt, his chest puffed out to twice its normal puffed-out size. "It would be an honor and a dream come true!"

They shook hands and walked off to discuss tactics.

We stood staring at one another, unable to believe what had just happened. Talk about dreams come true!

"I think this has been the best day of my life!" said Jack. "Not only did we win the Northwest interschool competition for the first time in forty-nine years, but we just got rid of Mr. Grunt . . . forever!"

Chapter 61

Fred and Clive's last stand

What a day! I don't like to take pleasure in anybody else's misfortune, but I couldn't help thinking that if ever a school deserved Mr. Grunt, it was Northwest West Academy. They were made for each other.

David and Fiona, returning from their victory lap, put the cup back down on the presentation table.

"Wow!" said Jack as we leaned in for a closer inspection. "Look at that! It must be made of solid gold!"

"Don't be ridiculous," said Fiona, who even in the midst of all the excitement could not stand for an inaccurate fact to go uncorrected. "It's a copper-tin alloy sprayed with gold paint."

"That's good enough for me!" boomed Gretel. "Can I hold it?"

"Sure," said Fiona, holding it out to her. "But be careful."

"Why?" said Jack. "It's just pure copper-tin alloy sprayed with gold paint!"

"It's still valuable," said Fiona. "And it's the only one we've got."

"Don't worry," said Gretel. "I'll be careful."

But before Gretel could take the cup from Fiona, there was a commotion behind us and a pair of skinny white arms reached out and grabbed it.

"I got it, Fred!" said the unmistakable voice of Clive Durkin.

"Well, don't just stand there!" yelled Fred. "Throw it to me!"

Clive hurled the cup over our heads to Fred, who was waiting on the edge of the group. Fred sprinted off toward the stadium exit. Clive took off after him.

"The cup!" yelled Gretel. "They've stolen our cup!"

While the rest of us milled around in confusion, Newton was in no doubt about what to do. He took off across the grass in hot pursuit.

"Wow!" said Jenny. "Look at Newton go!"

"Run, Newton, run!" yelled Mr. Brainfright, going back into mascot mode.

"New-ton Hoo-ton
Please speed up!
Catch those boys!
Bring back our cup!"

Whether it was Mr. Brainfright's chant, his program for sporting success, Newton's increased confidence, or a combination of all three, it was impossible to say. But the next thing we saw was Newton launching himself through the air to bring down both Fred and Clive in a spectacular tackle.

"He's got them!" said Gretel. "Quick! We've got to help him before they get away!"

Gretel's words woke us up out of our amazed stupor.

Fred was already doing his best to crawl out from underneath Newton when Gretel arrived and picked up both him and Clive by their shirt collars.

"You're not going anywhere," she said.

"Put us down right now!" demanded Clive. "Or else!"

"Or else what?" said Gretel.

"Or else I'll tell my brother!" said Clive. "And he's not going to be happy."

"I already know, you idiot!" said Fred. "And you're right! I'm *not* happy!"

"Neither am I!" said Gretel, tightening her grip on their collars.

By this time everybody else, including Mr. Brainfright and Principal Greenbeard, was crowded around us.

"Whose side are you on, anyway?" said Gretel. "Did you actually want Northwest West Academy to win?"

"No, of course not," said Fred. "We were just joking around, weren't we, Clive?"

"Yeah," said Clive, "just a little fun ... gee, lighten up."

"They're lying!" I said. "They've been working against us all along!"

"Mutineers?" said Principal Greenbeard. "Mutineers aboard the good ship *Northwest Southeast Central*? Why, that's terrible! I can scarcely believe my ears!"

"You don't have to," said Fred, shooting me a look of pure hatred, "because it's not true! Henry's making it up."

"No, I'm not, sir," I said. "I can prove it."

"Well, I think you'd better, Henry," said Principal Greenbeard. "Mutiny is a very serious offense and warrants the harshest punishment available to a ship's captain."

"Death?" said Jack hopefully.

"Walking the plank!" said Principal Greenbeard.

"Oh," said Jack with a sigh of disappointment.

"And then death!" said Principal Greenbeard. "How fast depends on how hungry the sharks are."

"All right!" said Jack enthusiastically. "Now you're talking!"

Jenny elbowed Jack. "Don't encourage him!" she whispered.

"Well, Henry?" said Principal Greenbeard.

"I wouldn't do this if I were you, McThrottle," Fred whispered. "I'll tell everybody about you-know-what."

"Tell them," I whispered back. "See if I care!"

"Oh, we'll see all right," said Fred.

"We're waiting, Henry!" said Principal Greenbeard.

I told him everything I knew. I told him about how Fred and Clive were big fans of Mr. Constrictor and how they'd known about the bus attacks, how they'd kept Mr. Constrictor informed about our mascot, which gave him time to train Chomp to attack bananas, and how they'd even threatened our own team that their heads would be squeezed if they won their events.

Principal Greenbeard was shocked. Fred had a reputation as one of the best and most responsible students in the school — as far as the teachers were concerned, anyway. The students, of course, knew better.

"Well, Fred?" said Principal Greenbeard. "These are very serious allegations. What do you and Clive have to say for yourselves?"

Fred tightened his mouth and stared at me. "Well, at least I didn't cause a tanker to skid off course and destroy the Banana Emporium and half of Northwest!" he said, looking at me the whole time.

"Don't be ridiculous!" said Fiona. "That wasn't *Henry's* fault. There was something wrong with the truck's brakes. Everybody knows that, duh!"

"But . . ." said Fred, looking confused, "I saw the whole thing. . . . Henry . . . and the banana suit . . . and . . . and . . ."

"My dad is an accident investigator," said Fiona confidently. "One of the best in the Northwest. He filed the report. It was a faulty brake line. End of story."

"But . . ." said Fred, looking confused, "but . . ."

"But we're not here to talk about me," I said. "We're here to talk about you, Clive, and Mr. Constrictor."

Fred looked angrily at me, then he turned and looked up at Principal Greenbeard. He scrunched his face up — like he was about to cry.

"So, Fred," said Principal Greenbeard, "are Henry's allegations true?"

"No!" said Fred. "We didn't do anything, I swear! Well . . . *we did* . . . but we were forced into it by Mr. Constrictor. He said that if Clive and I didn't tell him *everything* we knew, and do *everything* he said, then he would squeeze our heads until they popped. His track record left us no choice but to believe him. I'm really and truly sorry, Principal Greenbeard, but we were just so scared."

"It's okay, Fred," said Principal Greenbeard, patting Fred on the shoulder and giving him a handkerchief to dry the tears that he had managed to push out. "I

183

think we all know what sort of man Mr. Constrictor is. It doesn't surprise me at all to know that he's not above bullying and threatening innocent children in order to get what he wants."

"But Fred's not innocent!" I said. "And neither is Clive!"

"Nobody is completely innocent," said Principal Greenbeard, "but I think in this case Fred and Clive deserve the benefit of the doubt."

Fred and Clive nodded like angels to Principal Greenbeard and then turned and smirked at me.

Chapter 62

The truth about Mr. Grunt's Olympic career

"Well, I'm glad we got that sorted out," said Principal Greenbeard. "But I must admit, Mr. Grunt's defection to Northwest West Academy is still a terrible blow. He is the best gym teacher Northwest Southeast Central School has ever had. His training methods were cutting edge!"

"Oh, I wouldn't be so sure about that," said Flip, who had come down from his booth to join in the celebrations.

"What are you talking about?" said Principal Greenbeard. "Where am I going to get another gym teacher as qualified as Mr. Grunt? He was in the Olympics, you know!"

"I wouldn't be so sure of that, either," said Flip with a mischievous grin. "That man bends the truth more than a *bunch of snakes trapped in an S-bend*."

Jack nudged me. "I definitely got that one!" he whispered, grinning.

"I'm scared of snakes," whispered Newton. "And I don't like S-bends much, either."

"Are you saying that Mr. Grunt *wasn't* in the Olympics?" said Principal Greenbeard.

"No, certainly not!" said Flip. "He was in the Olympics, all right — selling *souvenir programs*!"

"He was a *souvenir program seller*?" said Principal Greenbeard. "As well as competing?"

"He never competed!" said Flip. "As far as I know, he only sold programs."

"Well," said Principal Greenbeard, "Olympic track record or not, he's still a first-rate gym teacher and, don't forget, he coached us to our first-ever victory today!"

"Yes, but after how many defeats?" said Flip. "Listen here, Principal Greenbeard. I've seen more track-and-field competitions than you've had salt-water soup for breakfast, and the truth is you won in *spite* of him being your gym teacher. The real reason you won today is Mr. Brainfright. He's the best banana mascot I've ever seen. Shoot, I'd go so far as to say he's the best *mascot* I've ever seen — and believe me, I've seen them all!"

Mr. Brainfright blushed. "That's very nice of you to say, Mr. Johnson, but I don't think I would go that far. A mascot is nothing without a talented team, and the students did an amazing job!"

"Yes," I said, "but only thanks to the Brainfright Program for Sporting Excellence!"

"What's that?" Flip asked.

186

I told him about the daily visualization sessions Mr. Brainfright had been conducting and how powerfully they had improved our performances.

"Now that's cutting-edge training!" said Flip, shaking his head in admiration and then turning to Principal Greenbeard. "If you don't appoint this man as the official new sports coach of Northwest Southeast Central School this very instant, Greenbeard, then you are *madder than a bunch of mad monkeys in a mad monkey house in mad monkey land!*"

Principal Greenbeard turned to Mr. Brainfright. "What do you say?" he asked. "Will you be Northwest Southeast Central's new sports coach?"

Mr. Brainfright smiled widely and nodded. "It would be a great honor," he said. "On one condition."

"Name it," said Principal Greenbeard.

"That I'm allowed to continue being 5B's class teacher," he said.

"Done!" said Principal Greenbeard, shaking Mr. Brainfright's hand.

We all breathed a huge sigh of relief.

And excitement.

With Mr. Brainfright in charge, and Mr. Grunt working for Northwest West Academy, victory was not only assured for next year, but for many years into the future.

"Give me a BRAIN!" I yelled.

187

"BRAIN!" yelled every Northwest Southeast Central student.

"Give me a FRIGHT!" I yelled.

"FRIGHT!" they yelled.

"Put them together and what have you got?"

"BRAINFRIGHT!" chanted the school. "BRAIN! FRIGHT! BRAIN! FRIGHT! BRAIN! FRIGHT! BRAIN! FRIGHT! BRAIN! FRIGHT!"

The entire stadium was shaking and echoing with the thunderous noise. The only people who were not enthusiastically chanting were Fred and Clive Durkin — they were only pretending to — and Jenny, who was shaking me violently by the shoulder.

"Stop, Henry!" she said. "Tell everybody to stop!"

"What's the matter?" I asked, raising my hands to silence the chant.

"You know as well as I do that Mr. Brainfright can't be the coach," she said.

"Why not?"

"Yes, why not?" said Principal Greenbeard.

"Because Mr. Brainfright has mascot madness!"

"Mascot madness?" said Mr. Brainfright. "Me?"

Fiona stepped forward and began a detailed clinical description of his strange banana-obsessed behavior over the previous few weeks. I had to hand it to her. She left no detail unturned.

Mr. Brainfright listened intently. "Well, well!" he said, "I've certainly heard of mascot madness, but I *never* thought it would happen to me. I know I was thinking a lot about bananas, but I certainly had no idea it was *that* bad."

"It was," said Gretel.

"Yes," said Jack. "You were really freaking us out."

"I was scared," said Newton.

"Never mind!" said Mr. Brainfright, putting a reassuring hand on Newton's shoulder. "I'm better now. Mr. Constrictor's squeeze must have shocked it out of me."

Jenny looked at him uncertainly. "How can we be sure?" she said.

"Let's ask him a few questions about bananas!" I said.

"Good idea, Henry!" said Fiona, consulting her notebook. She turned to Mr. Brainfright. "What common viral skin condition can be cured by bananas?"

Mr. Brainfright shrugged. "I don't know."

"What frequency of the color chart does yellow occupy?" said Fiona.

Mr. Brainfright shook his head. "I couldn't say."

"What is the third most popular flavor of milk at the school cafeteria?"

Mr. Brainfright shrugged again. "Beats me," he said. "Banana?"

"You're just guessing, aren't you?" said Fiona.

"I'm afraid so," said Mr. Brainfright. "You see? I'm completely cured!"

"How can we be really sure, though?" said Jenny, still not completely convinced.

"I know!" said Jack, pulling a container of banana-flavored milk out of his bag and holding it out in front of Mr. Brainfright. "Would you like a drink?"

We all held our breath.

We knew how Mr. Brainfright felt about banana-flavored milk. He'd made his feelings very clear on that point.

"Why," he said, "I don't mind if I do!"

He took the milk, tipped it up to his mouth, and drank the entire carton. When he finished, he licked his lips. "I sure needed that!" he said. "It was hot inside that suit!"

"You can say that again," I said.

Jenny nodded and smiled. "He's Mr. Brainfright, all right," she said.

"So you can be our new coach?" said Principal Greenbeard.

"With the greatest pleasure!" said Mr. Brainfright. "We will, of course, need a new mascot, though!"

This time I didn't have to think about it. My hand shot up. "I'll do it!" I said.

Chapter 63

The last chapter

Well, that's my story.

And just in case you're wondering, it's all true.

Every last bit.

If you're ever passing through Northwest, and you happen to be passing Northwest Southeast Central School, feel free to drop in.

We're pretty easy to find. Our classroom is the first on the left as you go up the steps.

And our teacher wears a purple jacket.

But don't forget to stop in at the office first and sign the visitors' book.

And while you're doing that, check out our winner's cup in our new glass cabinet. It's easy to spot — it's the only thing in there. But don't linger for too long because our office lady, Mrs. Rosethorn, doesn't like time-wasters.

Anyway, it would be great to see you, and if you enjoyed this story, then don't worry, I have plenty more!

And they're all true.

Every last one.

Chapter 64

Epilogue: The seven B's of banana mascotting

If you've been inspired to become a banana mascot yourself, here's a guide that tells you everything you need to know.

1. **Be big**

    Let them know you're there. Make a big entrance. Grab their attention. Remember, you are not a peach, or a cherry, or a tiny insignificant grape — you are a banana!

2. **Be careful**

    Watch out for uncovered manholes, escaped gorillas, and discarded banana peels. And remember to look both ways when crossing a road.

3. **Be exaggerated**

    You're in a huge costume — you need to double or even triple the actions you would normally do so your costume doesn't hide what you're doing. Marching is usually suggested; try not to drag your feet, but pick them up off the ground. A smooth wobble, a jump in your step, a fluid angry prowl, or even a childlike bounce add character to your steps. If you're waving to thousands, make sure the guy in the upper row can see you. Use your whole body.

4. Be emotional

Think about how emotional sporting events can get. Practice a number of emotions — happy, sad, angry, scared, excited — in front of a mirror with your banana head on. Learn where the facial features of your costume are and use them the way a banana would. Once you've perfected some emotions using your head and arms, try to use the rest of your body as well. Shivering, slow motion, trudging feet, tantrums, jumping up and down, and skipping are great moves to try.

5. Be respectful of people who don't like bananas

Believe it or not, not everybody goes bananas about bananas. If somebody is screaming and crying and threatening to call the police if you don't leave immediately, it's a good idea to leave immediately.

6. Be brilliant

Be the best banana you can possibly be. Remember, your team is depending on you.

7. Be careful

Don't spend too long in the suit at one time, and if you start to become overly fond of the color yellow or find that you can't stop talking or thinking about bananas, get somebody to give you a big shock.

FOR MORE NOSTRIL-BURNIN' FUN, JUST GET YOUR BUTT TO

WWW.SCHOLASTIC.COM/ANDYGRIFFITHS

- HOP TO SAFETY AND VICTORY IN THE ONE-AND-ONLY

ANDY GRIFFITHS GAME

- DISCOVER ANDY'S FAVORITE THINGS (LIKE FINDING **DIRTY TOOTHBRUSHES** AND ADOPTING THEM)

- READ **LAUGH-OUT-LOUD** EXCERPTS FROM SOME OF ANDY'S FUNNIEST BOOKS!

10,000 Volts of Lunacy — No Apologies

JOIN ANDY IN HIS QUEST TO SHOCK AND ANNOY EVERYONE AROUND HIM. BRACE YOURSELF—HERE COMES THE PLAYGROUND OF DOOM, GIRL GERMS, AND ANDY THE ROBOT. EACH MADCAP ADVENTURE IS MORE HILARIOUS THAN THE LAST. YOU'LL LAUGH SO HARD YOU'LL LOSE YOUR LUNCH.

◼SCHOLASTIC

WWW.SCHOLASTIC.COM/ANDYGRIFFITHS

SHOCKING

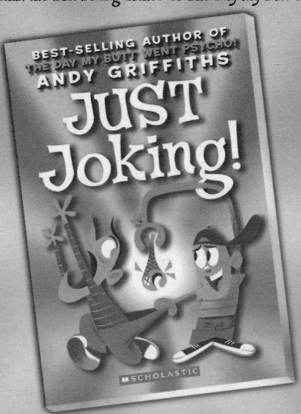